PENGUIN BOOKS

A GUIDE TO THE WESTERN FRONT

Victor Neuburg was born in Sussex in 1924 and educated at Varndean and at the universities of London and Leicester. At one time a soldier and schoolmaster, he is a former Senior Lecturer at the School of Librarianship, Polytechnic of North London. He has been a visiting professor at State College, Buffalo, Dalhousie University, Nova Scotia, and Ruhr University, Bochum. In the summer of 1984 he was Simon Foster Haven Fellow of the American Antiquarian Society. His previous publications include *Popular Education in Eighteenth Century England* (1971), *Popular Literature* (Penguin, 1977), and *The Batsford Companion to Popular Literature* (1982). He has also edited *Selections from London Labour and the London Poor* by Henry Mayhew for the Penguin Classics.

Victor Neuburg is married, with a wife inured to his enthusiasm for book collecting, and has a daughter and two granddaughters. He attributes his fascination with the First World War to his family: his mother had six brothers who served in all three of the services. None of them became a casualty.

Victor Neuburg

A Guide to
The Western Front

A Companion for Travellers

Penguin Books

This book is partly for Jim Wakeley who believed in it; partly for the 28th and 61st Regiments of Foot – now the Gloucesters – who were there; and mostly for Barbara, who was not . . . but knows why

PENGUIN BOOKS

Published by the Penguin Group
27 Wrights Lane, London w8 5TZ, England
Viking Penguin Inc., 40 West 23rd Street, New York, New York 10010, USA
Penguin Books Australia Ltd, Ringwood, Victoria, Australia
Penguin Books Canada Ltd, 2801 John Street, Markham, Ontario, Canada L3R 1B4
Penguin Books (NZ) Ltd, 182–190 Wairau Road, Auckland 10, New Zealand

Penguin Books Ltd, Registered Offices: Harmondsworth, Middlesex, England

First published 1988

Copyright © Victor Neuburg, 1988
The Illustration Acknowledgements on p. 10 constitute an extension of this copyright page
All rights reserved

Filmset, printed and bound in Great Britain by
Richard Clay Ltd, Bungay, Suffolk
Filmset in Monophoto Ehrhardt

Contents

Acknowledgements

Inevitably I have incurred a number of debts in the writing of this book. To Barbara Gilbert, who typed the manuscript, it is one which I am only too aware can never be adequately repaid.

Martin Gladman, Nigel Webber and Stanley Brett put books in my way. Brian Robertson always listened, and then commented perceptively. Staff at the Library of the Imperial War Museum were very helpful, and Tressell Publications made available some excellent illustrations. Thanks also to Mark Handsley of Penguin Books.

Many thanks to you all – and of course to my daughter Caroline, who toured the Salient with me.

Finally I must mention my long-suffering wife without whom, it is safe to say, this book would probably not have been completed . . . and I never did replace the pair of shoes she ruined while walking over Vimy Ridge . . .

Illustration Acknowledgements

The author and publishers would like to thank the following for permission to reproduce material:

Peter Carson for the photographs and other items on pp. 20, 23, 39, 107, 151, 155, 177, 182, 187, 192 and 225.

Leslie Coate of Tressell Publications for the diagrams on pp. 77, 148 and 149.

F. W. Jones (p. 21) for diagrams previously published in Nigel H. Jones, *The War Walk* (Robert Hale, 1983).

Ward Lock & Co. (pp. 12 and 74) for maps previously published in *Handbook to Belgium and the Battlefields*.

The Imperial War Museum (pp. 17, 19, 25, 26, 27, 51, 52, 57, 81, 91, 109, 113, 164, 173, 191 and 226) for photographs previously published in General Sir Ernest Swinton (ed.), *Twenty Years After. The Battlefields of 1914–1918* (1938).

All other illustrations are taken from the following publications by Bruce Bairnsfather: *Bullets and Billets* (pp. 37, 48, 55 and 126); *Fragments from All the Front* (p. 110); *Fragments from France* (pp. 29, 41, 45 and 120; *Still More Fragments from France* (pp. 90 and 101); and *From Mud to Mufti* (pp. 89, 131, 132, 167, 183 and 220).

A Note on Place-Names

Readers should be aware that there are often French and Flemish forms of place-names in Belgium. For simplicity's sake, most places in Belgium are referred to throughout this guide principally by their Flemish names, as given in the Michelin series of road maps recommended for use by the visitor to the Western Front (see p. 58). The differences between these and their French forms are slight.

In cases where the French form of a name would not easily be recognized from its Flemish version, French names are used in preference to Flemish as, generally speaking, they will be more familiar to English-speaking travellers from other literature. A list of these place-names is given below.

French	Flemish
Bruges	Brugge
Comines	Komen
Courtrai	Kortrijk
Gand	Gent (Eng. Ghent)
Liège	Luik
Lille	Rijsel
Messines	Mesen
Mons	Bergen
Passchendaele	Passendale
Tournai	Doornik
Ypres	Ieper
Yser (river)	IJzer

Dunkirk is generally referred to in its familiar English form in general text, but in its French form, Dunkerque, in the guide sections.

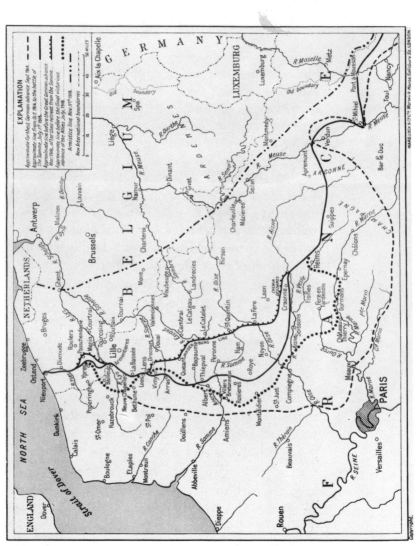

The battle lines of the Western Front 1914–18

Introduction

When the young men of Europe went to war in the late summer of 1914, many of them believed, so it was said, that they would be home by Christmas. In the event, the conflict spread beyond the frontiers of Europe, and increasingly large numbers of the world's inhabitants found themselves either directly or indirectly touched by it. Nevertheless, despite the near-universality of the armed struggle that lasted for over four years, it is the Western Front which is regarded today – and, indeed, was so regarded by many at the time – as the most important theatre of war. It was here that the German army was finally defeated. And the phrase 'Western Front' becomes even more evocative as the years pass.

To travel the landscapes of Flanders and northern France today is to be aware that these flat rolling plains and occasional low ridges and rivers have during the twentieth century become part of the British folk memory. Although their history stretches back to a remote antiquity, it is the few years between August 1914 and November 1918 that focus our attention and loom large, if often somewhat incoherently, in our thoughts. It is phrases like 'backs to the wall' and 'poor bloody infantry', and place-names such as Mons, Ypres and the

Somme, that stir memories. The Great War of 1914–18 was largely and decisively fought here, and in the epic struggle, in which so many national armies were involved, those of Britain and her colonies and dominions – as they were then called – played a distinguished part. Many were killed on those battlefields. Millions more were scarred both physically and mentally by the conflict. The history of the world was irrevocably changed by it.

Many of us may have, or have had, personal links with this far-off war – a father, grandfather, relative or friend who lived to tell the tale and whose anecdotes are still remembered. Equally, many of us will recall widows and maiden ladies whose husbands or sweethearts had been killed and whose presence within the family circle was always a reminder of what was very nearly a lost generation.

It is the dead who are remembered. Once a year we celebrate Armistice Day – though not with the seriousness and sense of loss which characterized the act of remembrance up to 1939. Imitation poppies symbolizing the sacrifice of the dead are worn, public dignitaries gather at the Cenotaph in Whitehall, and the nation – thanks largely to television – takes part in a vicarious act of homage to the dead of what are now two world wars. All this happens not on 11 November, the day when the guns fell silent in 1918, but on the nearest Sunday. This is presumably so that life can go on with as little interruption as possible. Thus the decencies of honouring the fallen are not overlooked, but simply moved to a more convenient time.

What relevance can such carefully rehearsed pomp and circumstance have to personal grief and to a national sense of loss at so appalling a waste of human life? It is inevitable, perhaps, that we ask this for the most part within the context of the years from 1914 to 1918, for this is the war which captures our imagination. After so many years, the immensity of human suffering, contrived by opposing states-men, continues to defy belief. No less than 12 per cent of the British adult male population became casualties, and other combatant countries suffered as badly if not worse. War memorials in towns and villages throughout the British Isles and Europe, and countries such as Canada, Australia and New Zealand, bear witness to the extent of the tragedy – and all this without taking into account the casualties suffered by the United States of America, which entered the war in 1917, or by the soldiers in op-posing armies . . .

It is difficult, more than two generations later, to be objective about the conflict. Feelings may still run high. The reputation, for example, of Field Marshal Haig, British Commander-in-Chief from 1915 to 1918, is still a matter of controversy, and opinions regarding his conduct of the war remain sharply divided. We might, on the one hand, ponder the extent to which political folly and military in-eptitude are redeemed by the courage of those who die or are mutilated in battle. On the other hand, it could be argued – though less cogently perhaps – that there was a hideous inevitability about events on the Western Front, and that given the situation of opposing armies, each well dug in and facing one another, fighting took on its own momentum and ran beyond anyone's control once battle was joined.

Leaving aside such contentious issues, there can be no doubt at all that the courage, endurance and sacrifice of the fighting soldiers are beyond argument. For whatever reason – and reasons there were many – they faced danger and hardship on a day-to-day basis, in most sectors of the Western Front, such as we can hardly imagine today. This book is a guide to their world some seventy years on. It is a much changed world, but it is well worth exploring. I have written for the non-specialist reader who finds himself or herself on the Continent, perhaps *en route* for a holiday further south, but who nevertheless is willing to spend a couple of days, or even somewhat longer, visiting the battlefields. It will also serve the purpose of the weekender who has an interest in the war. What it will not do is satisfy the demands of the dedicated military buff. Such a person is already splendidly catered for in Rose E. B. Coombs's *Before Endeavours Fade* (4th edn, 1983). It is a marvellous book, and I am greatly indebted to it.

What It was Like

Yea, how they set themselves in battle-array
I shall remember to my dying day.

John Bunyan

A visit to the battlefields of the Western Front may well prompt, apart from a range of generalized emotions running from anger to incomprehension, three fairly specific questions: What was it like to be there? How did men endure the horrors of the battlefield over so long a period? And what happened when the fighting stopped? The purpose of this section is to attempt an answer to these questions.

'Tension'. A private from the 1/4th E. Lancashire Regiment watches the German line through a periscope (note the way it is camouflaged to conceal it from the attention of enemy snipers). He is seated on his greatcoat at the head of a sap. (Sap was the term given to trenches dug outwards, to the front or rear, from existing lines. This one, used for observation, ran into no-man's land)

When we ask what it was like, what we really have in mind is how it was in the trenches. Infantry battalions were rotated on a regular basis – front line, support, 'rest' – and of course this brought differences of degree in the conditions that they had to endure.

Footsoldiers ('poor bloody infantry', or PBI, as they were called) going into the trenches were said to be going 'up the line', and those leaving them 'down the line'. These troops faced the enemy across a strip of territory, known as no-man's land, which could vary considerably in width from sector to sector. Here in the front line they faced shell, machine-gun, grenade, mortar and sniper's bullet on a daily basis, so that to the physical danger of sudden death or mutilation there was a background of constant noise – though, indeed, the word 'background' was often not appropriate, for at times the sound of guns could be heard in the south of

England. It has to be realized that, unless the troops were engaged in a raid or in a major battle, much of the time was passed in waiting; but such waiting, although tedious, was never passive. The trenches themselves, and the barbed-wire defences, always stood in need of repair; there was the eternal struggle to keep weapons clean in hideously difficult conditions; moreover, trenches were on full alert at dawn and dusk, when there would be 'stand-to' in case of enemy attack.

Then there were the discomforts of cold and mud,* lack of sleep, being unwashed, and indifferent food. To generalize about how it was in the front line is difficult – but not impossible. Against a background of shifting attitudes and memories, some things did not change. 'Mud, lice and rats compete for pride of place in my memory,' said one ex-soldier; and he went on to say about a spell on duty in the trenches during the night, when it might have been difficult to keep awake, that 'one was almost grateful to the lice whose attentions kept one occupied'.[1]

Food was a major preoccupation. Bully beef, biscuits, Tickler's plum and apple jam passed into legend; but there is no doubt that regimental cooks had a difficult and unenviable task. Occasionally they might experiment with, say, a mess of biscuits stewed with jam, but more usually they stuck to stew and tea (the latter always with the peculiar flavour that comes from using chlorinated water), since both could reach the troops before becoming

* Even in summer things were no better. Lice on human bodies became more active, and the thick khaki uniforms worn throughout the year did not help. It is all too easy to imagine the sheer nastiness of crowded trenches in hot weather . . .

'Luncheon is now being served'. March 1917. Men of the Lancashire Fusiliers in the trenches being served with hot stew from a container

quite cold. Cooking individual rations in the trenches presented problems. Fuel was scarce and there was little suitable shelter, so recourse was had to Primus stoves, which could, in a narrow trench, be so easily knocked over . . .

Ever present in men's lives, in the trenches and pervading the battlefield, was the awful stench of dead bodies, human excrement, unwashed humanity, and cordite and other chemicals. Many veterans of the war recalled this, though more usually in private conversation than in print. A fairly uncommon reference was made by F. Manning, who described 'a reek of mouldering rottenness in the air'.[2]

So the physical and mental strains of trench life – even when a soldier escaped wounding – were considerable, and they took their toll of both officers and other ranks. Many broke under them, but probably not as many as one might imagine. Before

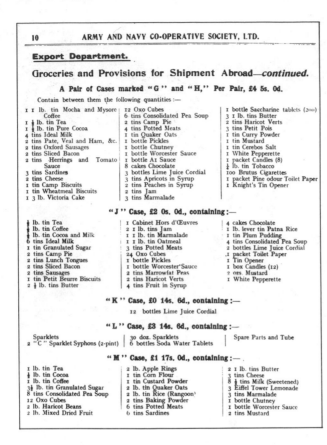

10   ARMY AND NAVY CO-OPERATIVE SOCIETY, LTD.

Export Department.

Groceries and Provisions for Shipment Abroad—*continued*.

A Pair of Cases marked "G" and "H," Per Pair, £4 5s. 0d.

Contain between them the following quantities :—

1 1 lb. tin Mocha and Mysore Coffee	12 Oxo Cubes	1 bottle Saccharine tablets (200)
1 ½ lb. tin Tea	6 tins Consolidated Pea Soup	3 1 lb. tins Butter
1 ½ lb. tin Pure Cocoa	2 tins Camp Pie	2 tins Haricot Verts
4 tins Ideal Milk	4 tins Potted Meats	3 tins Petit Pois
2 tins Pate, Veal and Ham, &c.	1 tin Quaker Oats	1 tin Curry Powder
2 tins Oxford Sausages	1 bottle Pickles	1 tin Mustard
2 tins Sliced Bacon	1 bottle Chutney	1 tin Cerebos Salt
2 tins Herrings and Tomato Sauce	1 bottle Worcester Sauce	1 White Pepperette
	1 bottle A1 Sauce	1 packet Candles (8)
3 tins Sardines	8 cakes Chocolate	½ lb. tin Tobacco
2 tins Cheese	3 bottles Lime Juice Cordial	100 Brutus Cigarettes
1 tin Camp Biscuits	3 tins Apricots in Syrup	1 packet Pine odour Toilet Paper
1 tin Wheatmeal Biscuits	2 tins Peaches in Syrup	1 Knight's Tin Opener
1 3 lb. Victoria Cake	2 tins Jam	
	3 tins Marmalade	

"J" Case, £2 0s. 0d., containing :—

½ lb. tin Tea	1 Cabinet Hors d'Œuvres	4 cakes Chocolate
½ lb. tin Coffee	2 1 lb. tins Jam	1 lb. lever tin Patna Rice
½ lb. tin Cocoa and Milk	1 1 lb. tin Marmalade	1 tin Plum Pudding
6 tins Ideal Milk	1 1 lb. tin Oatmeal	4 tins Consolidated Pea Soup
1 tin Granulated Sugar	3 tins Potted Meats	2 bottles Lime Juice Cordial
2 tins Camp Pie	24 Oxo Cubes	1 packet Toilet Paper
2 tins Lunch Tongues	1 bottle Pickles	1 Tin Opener
2 tins Sliced Bacon	1 bottle Worcester Sauce	1 box Candles (12)
2 tins Sausages	2 tins Marrowfat Peas	2 ozs. Mustard
1 tin Petit Beurre Biscuits	2 tins Haricot Verts	1 White Pepperette
2 ½ lb. tins Butter	4 tins Fruit in Syrup	

"K" Case, £0 14s. 6d., containing :—

12   bottles Lime Juice Cordial

"L" Case, £3 14s. 6d., containing :—

Sparklets	30 doz. Sparklets	Spare Parts and Tube
2 "C" Sparklet Syphons (2-pint)	6 bottles Soda Water Tablets	

"M" Case, £1 17s. 0d., containing :—

1 lb. tin Tea	2 lb. Apple Rings	2 1 lb. tins Butter
½ lb. tin Cocoa	1 tin Corn Flour	3 tins Cheese
1 lb. tin Coffee	1 tin Custard Powder	8 ½ tins Milk (Sweetened)
3½ lb. tin Granulated Sugar	2 lb. tin Quaker Oats	3 Eiffel Tower Lemonade
8 tins Consolidated Pea Soup	2 lb. tin Rice (Rangoon)	3 tins Marmalade
12 Oxo Cubes	2 tins Baking Powder	1 bottle Chutney
2 lb. Haricot Beans	6 tins Potted Meats	1 bottle Worcester Sauce
2 lb. Mixed Dried Fruit	6 tins Sardines	2 tins Mustard

Officers' messes supplemented army rations with extras for which they had to pay. The Army and Navy Stores offered various selections

leaving the trenches on a raid or during an offensive tensions ran high, and a rum ration was issued to steady men's nerves. Robert Graves described in graphic terms an episode at the outset of the Battle of Loos when three gallons of rum bubbled away into the mud, and what happened to the hapless soldier who was responsible for the loss.[3]

In close support, and sharing front-line conditions to a greater or lesser extent, were doctors, orderlies, stretcher-bearers, gunners, engineers. For them, too, it was a very tough war. For the increasingly large numbers of supply, support and

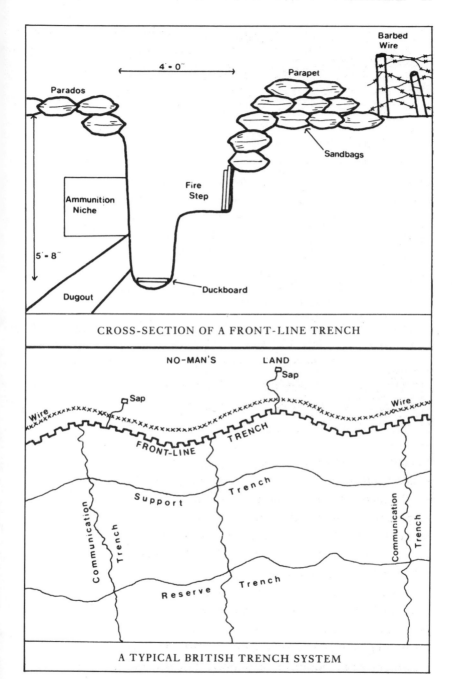

CROSS-SECTION OF A FRONT-LINE TRENCH

A TYPICAL BRITISH TRENCH SYSTEM

specialist troops behind the lines, things were not quite so bad. They were often derisively referred to as 'Base Wallahs', but ironically enough it was their skills and hard work which made life possible at the front. A private in the Army Ordnance Corps working at a base depot had a much easier time than his counterpart in the infantry, but if he was engaged upon repairs to lorries, ambulances or artillery pieces that would go back into service, who could say that his contribution was less vital? Staff officers at various headquarters attracted – with whatever justification, if any – the sharpest jibes. Siegfried Sassoon's bitter comment about 'Scarlet Majors at the Base' referred not only to their red lapel tabs of office but also to what he saw as their bibulous faces.*

Clearly this was unjust, and of course attitudes were more ambiguous than army slang and rhetoric might lead us to suppose, but an infantry officer returning to his battalion after some time away from it had his own ideas about the Staff, and at the same time a keen perception of change in the attitudes of front-line troops:

I rejoined my battalion in September, 1917, after an absence of ten months' bottle-washing on the Staff. It

---

* In 'Base Details', a poem first published in *Counter Attack*, Heinemann, 1918. The same kind of attitude is to be found in Shakespeare (*King Henry IV Part 1*, Act 1, Scene iii).

HOTSPUR   But I remember when the fight was done,
    When I was dry with rage and extreme toil,
    Breathless and faint, leaning upon my sword,
    Came there a certain lord, neat, and trimly dressed,
    Fresh as a bridegroom . . .
           . . .
    And as the soldiers bore dead bodies by,
    He call'd them untaught knaves, unmannerly.

was odd what ten months which included two major battles could do; they had changed the battalion completely. The battles of the Ancre and the fighting in front of Arras had swept away most of the remnants of the original Service Battalion. Headquarters and the transport were much the same, but in the companies was scarcely a face one knew.

Moreover the spirit of the battalion had changed. When we came to France in July, 1915, even when we went into the Somme in July, 1916, we were largely amateurs: very enthusiastic, and very inexperienced. In just over a year, the enthusiasm had vanished . . .[4]

Officers provided much of their own field equipment. This shows a selection of items offered for sale in October 1914 by the Army and Navy Stores

---

2 ARMY AND NAVY CO-OPERATIVE SOCIETY, LTD.

No. 4 Department.

FIELD EQUIPMENT.

The Society is anxious that purchasers should see that fair terms are being given, and is supplying a set of Field Equipment in two qualities, one at £7 10s., designated "A," and one at £5 15s., designated "B," details of which are given hereunder :—

Price of each Article.				Price of each Article.			
Improved " X " Bedstead	£1	18	0	Improved " X " Bedstead	£1	18	0
Bag	0	3	0	Bag	0	3	0
Pillow	0	4	9	Pillow	0	4	9
Bucket	0	3	0	Bucket	0	3	0
" X " Chair	0	7	3	" X " Chair	0	7	3
W.P. Sheet	0	12	8	W.P. Sheet...	0	12	8
" X " Bath and Basin ...	1	4	9	" X " Bath and Basin ...	1	4	9
Kit Bag to contain ...	3	3	6	Sack Bag to contain ...	0	15	6
				Table	0	12	0
	£7	**16**	**11**		**£6**	**0**	**11**
Per Set (as per Sealed Pattern)	£7	10	0	Per Set	£5	15	0

THE WAR OFFICE SEALED PATTERN IMPROVED " WOLSELEY " VALISE.

In Mail Canvas	...	...	...	...	£3	0	6
In Green Canvas	...	...	...	...	2	17	6

Once out of the line, men fared rather better during 'rest' periods. They would be accommodated in billets or in tents, and there was the chance of washing or showering, a change of socks and underwear, better food and perhaps some un-interrupted sleep. There were drawbacks, however. 'Rest' periods might be given up to days of intensive training for a new offensive, or to preparation for an inspection, perhaps by the General commanding the Division, when medals for gallantry might be presented. Sometimes a regiment would insist upon a near-peacetime routine, and this meant a ceremonial 'beating retreat' each evening. There would be church parades and guard duties; and almost certainly some time would be spent humping stores or trench equipment. These 'fatigues', as they were called, came round often, for the infantry were regarded as maids of all work. It was C. E. Montague, novelist and journalist on the old *Manchester Guardian*, who described the life of inf-antrymen so vividly when he wrote of

an image of that old trench life as the sum of innumerable units of irksome fatigue. This was the normal life of the infantry private in France. For NCOs it was lightened by the immunity of their rank from fatigue work in the technical sense. For the officer it was much further light-ened by better quarters and the servant system. For most of his time the average private was tired. Fairly often he was so tired as no man at home ever is in the common run of his work.[5]

Yet it would be a mistake to suggest that men in the front line, or just behind it, suffered a regimen of unrelieved misery. They did not, because the human spirit is remarkably resilient even under the most appalling conditions. There were always what might be termed 'the minor pleasures of war', which survivors, in after years, recalled with so keen a sense of warmth.

There would, for instance, be the arrival of letters and parcels from home – and the troops would have their own letters to write, too, though it should be remembered that these were subject to censorship. The importance of mail in keeping up morale was quickly realized. By 1 September 1914 all letters from troops in France and Belgium were carried free, and by June 1915 the volume of mail was such that four Base Army Post Offices had been opened in Channel ports.

'The Postman'. Somewhere in France, 1916. A gunner in the Royal Artillery brings the mail for his battery

Then there were diversions. Some formations and units organized concert parties or other entertainments: an example of this would be the production of *Cinderella* put on by a Kite and Balloon

Section of the Royal Flying Corps in January 1918, a photograph of which is held by the Imperial War Museum. Enterprises such as this were very much on an *ad hoc* basis, but there were more professional shows when performers came out from the U K. Organized sport was popular, and when units were out of the line football matches, boxing and athletics meetings would be arranged at battalion, brigade and divisional level. Football could be more informal than this, too. A story was told of a battalion which went into action at Loos dribbling a football between them as they advanced into enemy fire. More rarely there was cricket. Robert Graves remembered a game played between officers and sergeants some three quarters of a mile behind the front line. The bat was a piece of rafter from a ruined house and the ball a bundle of rags held together by string . . .[6]

Behind the lines, wine and beer, or 'Eggs, Chips, Fish, Tea', could be bought at *estaminets*, and

'The Opportunists'. A group of warrant officers and sergeants, mostly from the Army Service Corps, playing cards near Poperinge in 1917. Their 'table' is a short length of duckboard, thousands of which were used in trenches and on muddy ground all over the Western Front. (The A S C became 'Royal' in 1918 in recognition of their endeavours during the war)

'A Delicate Operation'. A British soldier buying fresh vegetables in Saint-Omer, July 1918. Sign language is clearly proving effective

YMCA and Expeditionary Force canteens were to be found in most areas. In some towns there were shops that did a roaring trade selling extras to men who wanted to add variety to an army diet. Always, however, the best establishments were clearly marked 'Officers Only'.

Such diversions helped to make life at the front more bearable than it would otherwise have been.

Almost all of them, it should be added, were of the kind taken for granted in time of peace, but two others require mention. The game of 'Crown and Anchor' or 'House', the only gambling permitted by the army, was widely played throughout the BEF* – and maintains a vigorous life today as 'Bingo'. And there was the pleasure – in many cases a keen and reciprocal one – of contact with French and Belgian civilians. Language was always a problem, but a basic French vocabulary of '*Combeeang?*', '*San fairy ann*', '*Bongjaw*', '*See voo play*', *au revoir* and *merci* could, and often did, work wonders in *estaminets*, shops and billets.

I have touched upon some of the minor pleasures that provided much-needed relief from the brutalities of war; but they were essentially palliatives, and the earlier question remains: how did men endure conditions at the front? To answer it we have first to distinguish between the old regular army and the new one made up of volunteers and conscripts who were serving for the period of hostilities only.† By the end of 1915 the old regular army and its reservists who had been recalled to

---

* The caller – usually a sergeant-major – used a language that could sound rather arcane to outsiders. 'Doctor's Shop', for example, was 9, a reference to the Number 9 Pill, which was a stock remedy employed by Medical Officers for men reporting sick with doubtful ailments.

† The dichotomy was not always as clear cut as we might suppose: there were survivors from the old army in the ranks of the new. Robert Graves described one of them in a poem as

> . . . an old stiff surviving
> In a New (bloody) Army he couldn't understand.

The whole poem ('Sergeant-Major Money') is worth reading as an indication of tragically conflicting attitudes. It is reprinted in I. M. Parsons (ed.), *Men Who March Away*, p. 61 (see p. 236).

their regiments in August 1914 had all but passed
into memory. Their ranks had been decimated at
Mons and at Ypres in 1914, and the Battle of Neuve-
Chapelle in 1915 virtually completed the process.

The problem of morale and steadiness in action was not a serious one for regular troops. In a carefully written and splendidly documented study,[7] John Baynes has shown how the 2nd Battalion Cameronians (Scottish Rifles) went into action on 9 March 1915 with a strength of about 700 officers and men. When they came out of battle six days later only a remnant of 143 men, commanded by a Second-Lieutenant, was able to parade for a roll call. Altogether thirteen officers and 112 other ranks had been killed, with the others wounded, many of them seriously. As Baynes says, with what must be deliberate under-emphasis: 'The 2nd Scottish Rifles was never again the same battalion . . .'[8] Numbers were made up with drafts of fresh reinforcements and the eventual return of wounded men, and the regiment lived on.

Such a record of loss and survival is in no way untypical of the regular army battalions. Each had a regimental tradition and a long-forged sense of loyalty to it that is, perhaps, hard for us to understand today, and it was this which led to steadfastness and courage in battle, to an acceptance of danger with no thought of saving oneself at the expense of others. It was a system, argued Baynes, that produced soldiers 'as near unconquerable as any . . . in the history of the world'.[9]

What, then, of the men who volunteered for service in the opening months of the war and who, together with the conscripts of 1916 onwards, took the place of regular soldiers in the ranks of a rapidly expanding army? For them, except in rare cases, regimental loyalty and tradition meant little. Yet, when the new men went into action at the Battle of the Somme in July 1916, and suffered appalling casualties (20,000 dead on the first day), they still went on to fight in other engagements, including the battle called Third Ypres just over a year later. These units did not break.* If we are to try to understand why, we must look beyond the notions of tradition and loyalty.

It is not too cynical to suggest that, from about mid-1916 onwards (precise dates are difficult to fix), battle-police stationed just behind the line during an offensive with orders to stop, interrogate, and if necessary shoot any unwounded man coming from the line played some part in preventing individual or even wholesale desertion in the face of the enemy. I do not believe, though, that this was a crucial issue, however important it may sometimes have been. The capacity of a group of men to show fortitude under enemy fire, suffer casualties and still advance is not created, or maintained, by the threat of force, still less by an oppressive discipline.

We must accept the fact that men were often extremely frightened; but what seemed important to so many of them was not to show this fear. The

---

* Individuals, however, did – and this can hardly be a matter for surprise. The following figures, taken from Anthony Babington, *For the Sake of Example* (see p. 234), show how many men were shot by firing squads in France and Belgium for desertion and cowardice:

> 1914 : 4
> 1915 : 48
> 1916 : 81
> 1917 : 87
> 1918 : 34

These are the numbers of executions traced, and represent 'worst cases'. The Australian authorities would never permit their men to be shot for these crimes – an attitude which irritated Haig who, in 1917, complained of Australian troops' indiscipline, but never, so far as I know, of their courage in battle.

Western Front was quite literally 'a man's world', and comparatively few, even under conditions of intolerable stress, would wish to appear to their

"Two minds with but a single thought, two hearts that beat as one."

fellows – or to their wives, girls and families at home – as anything less than a man doing a man's job in the front line. This was an idea buttressed by much propaganda of the time, and reflected something more than just self-esteem. At the same time it fell far short of a patriotic fervour and jingoism such as had characterized the early months of the war but which had dwindled as casualty lists lengthened.

For many men, too, joining the army could offer an escape from domestic responsibilities, from the drudgery of low wages, from long hours in dead-end jobs; it could offer relief from the anonymity of being simply another hand in the factory or on the farm, from being a shop assistant, from some repetitive and dreary clerical task. It was not too difficult to be a good soldier, and provided that one escaped death or wounding there was always the possibility of promotion to corporal, to sergeant, and even beyond to commissioned rank. This would mean higher pay and status, a heightened sense of individuality, and above all some authority, some responsibility for the doings of others. Even the most junior lance-corporal in battle might have to make life or death decisions. Peacetime occupations could not, in general, match this heady and – to some – attractive mixture of action, personal advancement and risk.

Overall, the BEF was an efficiently administered and well-supplied army. Despite lapses in the front line for which no one person could be held culpable, it was adequately (if unimaginatively) fed; medical care was excellent; home leave was on a fairly regular basis. All these elements, combined with some others that have been briefly mentioned, helped to maintain it as a coherent force under conditions in the field which no other British army had ever been called upon to face over so long a period . . . and we should not forget that it was ultimately victorious.

Victory, however, brought problems for the BEF, for the army at large and for Great Britain. The Armistice of 11 November 1918 was initially greeted with some scepticism by troops on the Western Front. There had been talk of peace on other occasions – but, at last, here it was. The Allies halted their advance, and the Germans withdrew out of sight and out of range. Disengagement of the opposing sides brought relief from the mental and nervous tensions of a long war, but the troops who had been rapidly advancing in the wake of the German retreat were too tired for any junketing, and such celebrations as there were in the war zone seem to have been muted. On the morning of 11 November, so tradition has it, artillery batteries had opened up early and vied with each other for the distinction of having fired the last shell; but at 11 a.m. everything fell silent. At a hospital near Étaples a medical officer on duty signed an order which read as follows: 'To celebrate the conclusion of hostilities every patient will be allowed an extra piece of bread and jam with his tea.'[10]

When the war ended there were some $3\frac{3}{4}$ million men serving in the army. By the end of 1919 approximately 3 million of them had been demobilized; but to quote these figures suggests a very much smoother operation than was in fact the case. The run-down of the army – always a more complex process than expansion – was to prove a very thorny issue. Only days after the fighting stopped, planners in London identified as a major problem the need to maintain recruitment for the army. 'There was a risk', said Lord Milner, Secretary for War, 'of the government being without any army at all in 6 months!'[11] It was a timely warning. Much of Europe was still in turmoil, and the British army still had its traditional commitment to finding large numbers of troops for Empire garrisons. There was the need to supply forces for the occupation of certain areas in Germany. And there was also the very real possibility – though in the end it came to nothing – of sending more units to Russia to reinforce the comparatively small number of British troops there in order to mount an intervention against the Bolshevik revolution. Men were still needed in Ireland, and it was possible that troops might have to be used on the streets of Britain to break strikes and to counter civil unrest.

Against this background the mood of most men who had served during the war was unequivocal: they wanted to go home. In this they were supported by the popular newspapers of the day. 'Send the boys home,' cried the *Daily Herald* on 7 December 1918. Why was there any delay? There were some who had reservations. Senior officers in the army, for instance, might understandably be ambivalent about a winding down. There is always a reluctance on the part of those who wield authority to surrender any part of it without some heart-searching, and high-ranking officers were certainly no exception. Settling back into a much reduced peacetime army – assuming that they were fortunate enough not to have been retired – would mean for most of them a reduction in rank, pay and status; and this could apply not only to senior officers but equally to many who held lesser rank. An uncle of mine was a regular soldier before the war, and during it became a captain in the Royal Norfolk Regiment commanding a rifle company in the line. After it he lost his commission and went to another regiment with a lesser rank.

During the war, when men perforce went dirty and military etiquette was not always punctiliously observed, many regular officers may have sighed for a return to what they saw as 'real soldiering', equated for them with spit and polish, kit inspections and regular parades. When finally hostilities ceased, things looked rather different. For a majority of men the feeling seems to have been that their obligations had been fulfilled and they were now civilians in khaki. This led not so much to a general relaxation of army discipline as to a growing unwillingness on the part of men to submit to it. From this sentiment, coupled with sheer ineptness on the part of the government in its initial handling of demobilization, there arose acts of collective indiscipline in the army – not excepting the BEF.

In Europe problems were exacerbated by the concentration of large numbers of men and by the urgent need to clear the fighting zone of its debris. In the form of unexploded shells, cartridges, landmines, barbed wire and the like, such debris constituted a continuing threat to the labour units engaged upon the task – no less than to a civilian population that was desperate to return to shattered farms, villages and towns.

The first major signs of disaffection in the BEF after the Armistice were manifested in Calais. In addition to the thousands of men permanently stationed there in supply, store and repair depots,

there was by January 1919 a shifting population of troops from virtually every unit in the army passing through the port on the way to or from Great Britain. Discontent developed into strike – and striking soldiers were hitherto unheard of in the army. It should be said that senior officers handled various incidents here with great care. Brigadier-General Wroughton, Commandant of the Calais Base, convened a meeting of soldiers, and their grievances were listened to.[12] Similar outbreaks occurred in camps in England, among them Folkestone, Osterley Park and Park Royal near London, Aldershot, Bedford, Leeds, Bristol . . .[13] January 1919 seems to have been the worst month for this unrest. On the 6th of that month about 400 men stationed at Uxbridge in Middlesex broke out of camp and marched along the High Street singing 'Britons never shall be slaves' and 'Tell me the old, old story'. In the marketplace they were addressed by their commanding officer, and they marched back. One of the men spoke to a reporter, complaining of slow demobilization and bad food, and eventually they

sent a deputation to the War Office.[14] Even at
Kantara, a huge base in Egypt, there was trouble.
Sapper Mills of the Royal Engineers wrote in his
diary for 28 January:

At night a meeting of protest as to the way we were
being treated over demobilization was held, the O.C.
[Officer Commanding] was present. Some strong
comments were made . . .[15]

These soldiers had served their country well. While
hostilities continued, a dogged resolution remained
in the ascendant. Afterwards, when men felt that
they were being unjustly treated, they were less
ready to make sacrifices.

There is one tragic footnote to the demobilization
story. In the churchyard of Bodelwyddan Church
near Rhyl in North Wales there are the graves of
eighty-three Canadian soldiers who were stationed
at nearby Kinmel Park Camp on their way home
from France. Some of them, according to local
memory, were shot by other Canadians during
troubles at the camp in 1919. There were repeated
delays in providing ships for the return journey, and
the camp became overcrowded . . . On one of the
gravestones is the epitaph: 'Some day, some time,
we will understand.'

That time has not yet, I suspect, arrived.

Finally, the army was required to serve as an Army
of Occupation in Germany. British troops arrived in
Cologne on 7 December 1918 and remained there
until 1926, three years before the last of the British
occupation forces left the country. French, American and Belgian contingents were stationed in other
areas of Germany, and in 1923 Franco-German

Cologne – British Forces in Cologne after the war

bitterness led to the sending of French troops into the Ruhr industrial district. The British occupation, however, was a fairly good-humoured affair.

Cologne attracted many distinguished visitors, among them Haig, Foch, Winston Churchill, Joffre and Henry Wilson, and the army had an important ceremonial role to play on such occasions. For the most part, though, time hung heavily for the troops, and strenuous efforts were made to keep them occupied and entertained. There were an 'Army College', organized sport and a daily newspaper (the *Cologne Post*) published by the Rhine Army, as well as concert parties like 'The Crumps', 'The Colognettes', 'The Tabs' and 'The Thistles', and a more serious theatre run by Esmé Percy, who was later to achieve fame on the West End stage and in films.

On 31 January 1926, as a result of representations made by Germany under the terms of the Peace Treaty and subsequent negotiations, the last members of the occupying force left the city for their new quarters at Wiesbaden. Cologne became a wholly German city once more, and today no trace of the British occupation remains.

It was in Wiesbaden that the final act of British military involvement in the Great War in Europe was played out. The last unit of the occupying forces, the 2nd Battalion The Royal Fusiliers, was withdrawn at the end of 1929. Just before its departure, on 12 December, Regimental Sergeant-Major Saunders lowered the Union Jack that flew outside British Headquarters. Then, with the band at its head followed by RSM Saunders and Sergeant Mawby – bemedalled veterans both – each carrying a colour over his arm, the battalion marched to the station and entrained for home – fifteen years and a few months after the first elements of the BEF had come ashore at Boulogne.

The Army

RANKS

Whatever the shared experience of comradeship in the trenches or under fire may have been, it is misleading to make too much of this unity between all ranks. The army as an institution did not recognize it, and would under no circumstances have

NO POSSIBLE DOUBT WHATEVER

SENTRY: "'Alt! Who goes there?"
HE OF THE BUNDLE: "You shut yer — mouth, or I'll
— come and knock yer — head off!"
SENTRY: "Pass, friend!"

approved its manifestations. Indeed, the palpable distinction between those who held the King's commission and those who did not was, in terms of uniform and style of living, absolutely fundamental to the running of the British military machine. The army made this explicit in the phrase 'officers and other ranks'. In 1914 the gulf between the two, while not impossible to bridge, was extremely wide.

One man who did cross the gap with spectacular success was Sir William Robertson. He enlisted in the ranks in 1877 and in due course was promoted corporal, sergeant and sergeant-major. Subsequently he was commissioned, and the outbreak of war found him Director of Military Training at the War Office. He served as Chief of the Imperial General Staff from 1915 to 1918, being made a Field Marshal in 1920. It was said of him that he was the only man in the British Army who had climbed all the rungs of the military ladder.

As the war went on, more and more officers were required to replace those who had become casualties, and increasingly men from the ranks were selected to undergo cadet training and become second-lieutenants. Many, of course, jumped at the chance; others were less sure of taking this step, and attitudes were often ambivalent. One anonymous private soldier in the winter of 1917 remembered his platoon officer approaching him: 'Look here, you seem an intelligent sort of fellow,' he said, explaining that he had been asked whether he had any men he could recommend for commissions. The soldier had misgivings about applying, and seems to have done so partly because a close friend had been approached too and partly because the training would mean at least three months in Blighty.* And, as he said, 'the possibility of being live officers rather than dead soldiers in the immediate future was tempting to consider at this stage of the war'. The two friends were rather ashamed to be leaving their comrades, and they loathed the cadet battalion; but both made it to Second-Lieutenant, and both survived the war.[16]

The highest rank in the army was Field Marshal, followed in descending order of seniority by General, Lieutenant-General, Major-General, Brigadier and Colonel. It is very unlikely that fighting soldiers would have had much contact with such exalted figures except on highly formalized occasions when decorations for gallantry were distributed, or on a special parade when they might be inspected, exhorted or − more rarely − praised.

The most senior officers to know the men by name, and in normal times something of their family background, would be the Lieutenant-Colonel and the Major, who were respectively the Commanding Officer and the second-in-command of an infantry battalion. Then, in each of the rifle companies into which the battalion was divided, other officers who would come, while on duty, into even closer contact with the men would be the Captain and subaltern officers, Lieutenant and Second-Lieutenant. As the anonymous private soldier quoted above put it in a rather jaundiced way:

---

* Britain, home. (Hindustani: *bilāyati*, a foreign land.) Formerly an everyday word with the army in India. Very early in the war it came into general currency and was used with many applications. A 'Blighty one', for example, was a wound which required its recipient to be sent home for treatment.

It was your platoon officer who mattered. The rest
you scarcely saw. The colonel – well some of our men did
not even know his name. As for the generals, it was
known that they existed; at rare intervals, usually at posh
inspections, they were caught sight of. But they cannot
be said to have impinged very sharply on the conscious-
ness of the private soldier. The higher command was
never mentioned.[17]

At the outset of the war officers wore their badges
of rank on the sleeves of their tunics; but, since this
made them conspicuous targets for enemy fire, the
practice grew up in the trenches of wearing rank
badges on the shoulders where they would be less
easily recognized from a distance. In 1917 the
change was made official and badges of rank could
be worn on cuff or shoulder. In 1920 cuff badges
were abolished. Before these decisions, however,
some regular battalions were resistant to the change.
When Lieutenant Robert Graves reported to the
2nd Battalion Royal Welch Fusiliers near Laventie
at the end of July 1915, he wore shoulder stars
indicating his rank. Over lunch the second-in-
command, a choleric officer, commented that he
was wearing a 'wind-up' tunic and asked: 'Why the
hell are you wearing your stars on your shoulder
instead of your sleeve?' Graves replied that he
thought it was the custom in France, but was ordered
to report to the regimental tailor to have cuff badges
sewn on immediately.*

Amongst other ranks the most senior was the
Regimental Sergeant-Major, almost always a remote

---

* *Goodbye to All That*, p. 109 (see p. 235). To have or get the 'wind
up' or to be 'windy' meant to be nervous or cowardly. The usage
originated in the army in about 1915.

LEAVE

Dep.: Paddington 2.15. Arr. Home 4

figure. Then there were other sergeants–major, quartermaster-sergeants and sergeants. These 'senior ranks', as they were called, lived apart from the men wherever possible and took their meals in the Sergeants' Mess. Corporals, lance-corporals and private soldiers, who formed the bulk of the army, lived a communal life in which any kind of privacy was hard to achieve.

Oddly enough, these systems worked remarkably well, because there was a strong sense of regimental tradition and, in the infantry, which recruited its men on a regional basis, a feeling of local loyalty, the focus of which was usually the county which gave the regiment its name. Both of these factors came under considerable pressure during the war, but both survived, even if in a somewhat attenuated form. At one time, for example, a number of 'pals battalions' were raised in which the volunteers received a firm undertaking that they would serve in the same regiment alongside their friends. The history of such battalions provides an illuminating example of the British genius for improvisation in time of crisis.

When hostilities began there was an immediate need for men and, on the crest of a wave of jingoism and popular sentiment, volunteers flocked to recruiting offices. In September 1914, 416,901 enlisted in the army (this was in fact the highest monthly recruiting total of the entire war), and an enormous strain was put upon regimental organization up and down the country. Partly to alleviate this and partly to stimulate recruitment the War Office had, as early as 12 August, originated a scheme for raising units from men with a common occupational background or a strong local link. Nine days later a 'Stockbrokers' battalion (10th Royal Fusiliers) began to recruit, and this was followed in September by a battalion raised by the North Eastern Railway. Another was sponsored by Glasgow Corporation Tramways . . . and the idea spread. Amongst these units raised by appeals to local feeling were the 'Grimsby Chums', the 'Oldham Comrades', the 'Tyneside Scottish' and the 'Tyneside Irish'. A regiment of 'Manchester Scottish' failed, apparently, to attract enough men and was merged with another unit; while another failure was the projected 'Merioneth Pals', who hoped to attract 'religious young men' – but nobody followed up this suggestion.

Battalions of infantry raised on the 'pals' principle wore the badges of established regiments: the 'ist Bradford Pals', for example, were the 16th Battalion, West Yorkshire Regiment, while the 'Hull Commercials' were the 10th East Yorks. There was a 'Sportsman's Battalion' raised by Mrs Cunliffe-Owen, and their camp at Hornchurch in Essex was built in nineteen days. In one of its huts, so it was said, 'one bed was occupied by the brother of a peer and the next by the man who drove his car . . .' It was envisaged that the Sportsmen (23rd Royal Fusiliers) should have in its ranks 'upper- and middle-class men', but this ideal was never realized, so chauffeurs, sailors and mechanics were accepted.

Altogether 115 infantry battalions (to say nothing of artillery batteries) were raised in this way, and eighty-three of them began life in 1914. The north of England was the most successful, with Lancashire and Cheshire totalling twenty-four battalions, Yorkshire fifteen and north-east England fifteen, while London raised twenty-three battalions. Some degree of latitude was given to those who initiated these units when it came to the matter of appointing officers, so great was the shortage of experienced men; and on occasion recruits continued to live at home during training because organizers had to make their own arrangements for housing the men they raised during the winter months of 1914–15.

Dependence upon voluntary methods of recruiting ended finally when the Military Service Act became law in January 1916. This made provision for the conscription of all single men and childless widowers between the ages of eighteen and forty-one. It was followed by six further amending Acts, and compulsory military service remained in force until 30 April 1920.

"Someone's been at this blinkin Strawberry"

FORMATIONS

The pre-1914 army was a small one: at the outbreak of war about 200,000 men were serving in it. When the war finished, more than $5\frac{1}{2}$ million men had served. The basis for this tremendous expansion was the 1914 organization of the army, which proved, with some modifications dictated by the immediate circumstances of war, to be remarkably flexible. There were then twenty-eight regiments of cavalry, four regiments of foot guards and sixty-nine infantry regiments, together with artillery, supply services, field ambulances and hospitals.

Of the sixty-nine infantry regiments, all except one (the Cameron Highlanders) consisted of two battalions with about 1,000 men in each; and the great expansion of the infantry took place upon the basis, initially, of the established regiments raising further battalions throughout the war. The Northumberland Fusiliers raised fifty-two; the Royal Fusiliers (City of London Regiment) forty-seven; the Welch Regiment thirty-four; the Devonshire Regiment twenty-five; and so on.

Four battalions were then grouped together to form a *brigade.**

Three brigades were grouped together to form a *division*. The division was a self-contained fighting force with its own artillery and support services. In theory its strength was 20,000 men of all ranks, but this varied with casualties. Because divisions quite often fought together, there are several divisional memorials on the Western Front.

Two, or occasionally more, divisions would be grouped together to form a *corps*.

A group of two or more corps would be designated an *army*.

Clearly there is some ambiguity about the term 'army', which is both a constituent element in the Armed Forces of the Crown and a battlefield formation. It can be resolved if we remember that the forces fighting in France and Flanders were

* In January 1918 brigades were reduced from four battalions to three.

called the British Expeditionary Force (BEF), which consisted eventually of five armies. The term 'army' in this sense was introduced on Christmas Day 1914, when two armies were formed by grouping the existing army corps in the field. In September 1916 the BEF was divided into five armies, an organization which lasted for the rest of the war. Control was exercised by the Commander-in-Chief at General Headquarters (GHQ) and his staff.

It was customary to refer to the armies in capital letters, e.g. THIRD ARMY; to corps with Roman numerals, e.g. XII Corps; and to divisions with Arabic numerals, e.g. 6th Division.

Such an organization gave rise to a large number of army, corps and divisional signs in various colours, which were worn on the sleeve, just below the shoulder, by all ranks. They carried a distinctive meaning for all concerned with each formation, and their purpose was threefold: they made recognition easier, they contributed to a feeling of *esprit de corps*, and they confused the enemy. The Australian and Canadian divisions mostly had geometrical patterns, but the British signs were more colourful. The 33rd Division, for example, had a double-three domino; XVII Corps, commanded by General Sir T. D'O. Snow, had a polar bear standing on an iceberg with the seven stars of the Great Bear constellation above; the Guards Division had an eye. There is a very good collection of these signs in the Imperial War Museum in London.

A FEW FIGURES

Two images probably characterize our picture of the Great War: khaki uniforms and steel helmets.

'Tin Hats'. Men of the King's Liverpool Regiment in the front line during April 1916. They are wearing newly acquired steel helmets, general issue of which had begun in the preceding month

The Battle of Majuba Hill in 1881 during the First Boer War was a resounding defeat for the British, who sustained a large number of casualties. One reason for this was the fact that the scarlet coats worn by the infantry made them conspicuous targets for the Boer sharpshooters who, wrote Captain Thurlow of the 3/60 Rifles in a letter after the engagement, 'poured a tremendous fire into our unfortunate men . . . knocking them over like rabbits'.[18] Following this disaster khaki uniforms were introduced into the army in India in 1885. They were universally worn by British troops in the Second South African War, and proved eminently more serviceable than scarlet in hard campaigning over unfriendly terrain; and in 1902 they became standard issue throughout the army.

The first 300,000 steel helmets were delivered to the army by the middle of March 1916, after some experimenting with design and material during the previous year.

Soldiers in the front line often had harsh things to say about the Staff at GHQ, and no doubt many of them were deserved; but it is worth recalling the scale and the scope of administrative operations by the end of the war. It was responsible for running a system which supplied a vast range of goods, from a tin of dubbin to a 15-inch howitzer. It ran a transport system comprising 500,000 horses and 20,000 motor lorries, besides 250 trains a day. It supervised the building of roads and railways and developed harbour facilities. There was also a complete medical and veterinary service.

'Repairing Guns'. A Warrant Officer in the Army Ordnance Corps supervising the repair of field guns at a travelling workshop near Amiens in April 1918. Later in the same year the AOC became 'Royal' in recognition of its work during the war

*China on the Western Front**

As the fighting in France and Flanders went on, ever greater quantities of stores, equipment, vehicles and ammunition had to be shipped from British ports to the war zone, unloaded and stored in dumps and depots. There were, too, camps and railway lines to be built and roads to be kept in a constant state of repair. To cope with these heavy tasks special labour units were formed, with British labourers, Africans, Indians, Egyptians, Fijians, German prisoners of war ... but above all there was the Chinese Labour Corps.

Lieutenant-Colonel Bryan Fairfax had left the army as a captain in May 1914, but rejoined at the outset of the war and was put in command of this Corps towards the end of 1916. Altogether some 100,000 Chinese workers were brought to Europe by the British authorities, and this was despite efforts made by the German Embassy in Peking to stop the recruitment of men who were in fact natives of a neutral country. The first of them left Shantung in January 1917 *en route* for France, which they reached in April. Disembarking at Le Havre, they went by rail to a camp at Noyelles-sur-Mer.

Most of the labourers had been enlisted in Weihaiwei, a small town in the Shantung province that the British had leased from the Chinese government in 1898. When they enrolled they declared themselves to be volunteers, and were deemed subject to military law. A wristlet with the

* This is the title of an excellent book by Michael Summerskill, published by the author in 1982. I have drawn heavily upon it in this brief account.

owner's personal number was riveted to every wrist and pigtails were cut off. Although pay was low by European standards even then, it was about four times what the men might have expected to earn at home, and thus there was an incentive to join the Labour Corps. The lowest rank amongst them earned one franc a day, while a Class One Ganger, Class Two Ganger and Class Three Ganger (relating roughly to sergeant, corporal and lance-corporal) earned proportionately more.

The language problem was considerable, and was only to some extent eased by the commissioning of missionaries, sons of missionary families or men who had been in business in Shantung and who knew something of the local dialect. There were also Chinese interpreters (non-commissioned, of course) who could earn up to 5 francs a day. Another problem – so it was perceived in those far-off days – was that of segregating the Chinese from British Army canteens, local civilians and, above all, women. It was one common, during the Great War, to the handling of all non-white labourers, and the solution was to keep the men in their camps when they were not working. Given the nature of British colonialism, this problem of segregation took on a peculiar urgency for the few non-European labour units stationed in this country.

At the foot of the North Downs, by Sugar Loaf Hill and Caesar's Camp near Folkestone in Kent, there was a camp to accommodate 2,000 Chinese and African labourers. It was officially Cherry Garden Camp, but unofficially it was known as 'Labour Concentration Camp'. In the nearby military cemetery at Shorncliffe there are the graves of six Chinese workers.

Such graves – and there are some two thousand of them in France, in many cemeteries where Europeans and non-Europeans lie side by side – add an especial poignancy to memories of the Chinese presence amongst the BEF. There were in all thirty-two camps that housed Chinese labourers, and at seven of them – Audruicq (Pas-de-Calais), Boulogne, Calais, Dieppe, Dunkirk, Noyelles-sur-Mer (Somme) and Tournhem (Pas-de-Calais) – the Chinese were at work for two or three years. There were Chinese hospitals as well.

Besides showing ingenuity and a remarkable capacity for sustained hard work these men, largely isolated from the world outside, imposed the pattern of their own culture upon the camps in which they lived. Today, except for their graves, there is little sign that they were ever here. At Noyelles-sur-Mer, their base depot and largest camp, there is a Chinese cemetery with a Chinese-style portico where 838 men are buried. The headstones – most of them without names, and with numbers usually the sole means of identification – bear one of four different inscriptions:

'A Noble Duty Bravely Done'
'A Good Reputation Endures For Ever'
'Though Dead He Still Liveth'
'Faithful Unto Death'.

The cemetery stands among cornfields at L'Argilière, north of the road from Noyelles to Sailly-le-Sec, about 12 km. north-west of Abbeville.

General Information

Getting There

No guidebook today need tell travellers how to cross the Channel. Information – details, for example, of new ferry services – is readily available from travel agents or the motoring organizations, who are well able to keep up to date with such matters.

It is a safe general rule that when you travel, especially in the peak summer season, you should make advance reservations.

The following information may be useful.

Ferries
P & O Ferries, Dover	tel. 0304 203388
Sally, The Viking Line, Ramsgate	tel. 0843 595522
Sealink, Dover	tel. 0304 240028

Hovercraft
Hoverspeed, Dover	tel. 0304 240202

Railways
Belgian National Railways, London Office	tel. 01-734 1491
French Railways, London Office	tel. 01-409 1224
Sealink UK, London	tel. 01-834 8122

Travellers are warned that, because the battlefields are usually away from the normal tourist routes, accommodation beyond the coastal resorts, or in Ypres, Poperinge, Amiens, Arras or Reims, may prove a little difficult. Belgian and French Tourist Offices are able to supply lists of approved hotels, but few of them are of three- or four-star grading. There are plenty of campsites.

The new motorways criss-cross the old battlelines, so the best way to see the battlefields is to stay on the older roads, most of which would have been known to the BEF. These comprise *Routes Nationales* (N), *Chemins Départementaux* (D or CD), and *Vicinaux Ordinaires* (VO). Travellers are warned that road numbers are prone to alteration, and that new roads are constantly being built. The author refers throughout this guide to maps available at the time of writing (see p. 58).

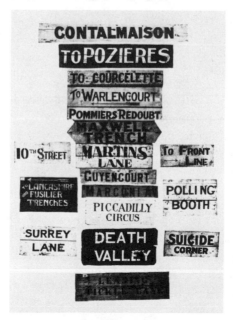

'Road and Trench Signs'. Some road and trench signs used in the battle areas

Maps

There are five Michelin 1:200,000 scale road maps covering the main areas of the fighting. These are:

Map 51: BOULOGNE/LILLE
Covers Ypres, Loos, Passchendaele, Messines, Vimy, Mons, Dunkirk, Calais, Béthune, the region north of Arras.

Map 52: LE HAVRE/AMIENS
Covers Amiens, south of Arras, Battle of the Somme (Canadian raid on Dieppe in the Second World War).

Map 53: ARRAS/CHARLEVILLE–MÉZIÈRES
Battle of the Somme, Arras, Cambrai, Saint-Quentin, Albert, Mons, Valenciennes.

Map 56: PARIS/REIMS
Covers important battle areas, particularly the German advance on Paris in 1914.

Map 57: VERDUN/WISSEMBOURG*
Covers one of the most bloody battles of the war.

* See p. 185 for details of a larger-scale map showing the Verdun battlefields.

It should be noted that these are not historical maps of the campaigns, and the roads shown on them are modern.

Copies of maps 51, 52 and 53, overprinted to show the precise location of each military cemetery and memorial, may be obtained from the Commonwealth War Graves Commission (see p. 61 for address).

Accommodation and Food

Most of the battlefields are not on normal tourist routes. Both the French and the Belgian National Tourist Offices will supply lists of hotels; and so far as the Salient is concerned, Ypres is the natural centre, offering a good selection of moderately priced hotels.

In France station restaurants are excellent and the *buffets de gare* offer good value for money. Some of the larger stations have more than one restaurant, catering for different tastes and pockets.

So far as self-catering is concerned, admirable bread can be bought in every French village (except between the hours of 12 and 2 p.m.). The hypermarkets that have sprung up in increasing numbers close to the larger towns offer a range of reasonably priced food and drink.

The situation is not quite so good in Belgium, but is improving.

The Commonwealth War Graves Commission (CWGC)

In 1917 the Imperial War Graves Commission was established, and the name was changed to its present form in 1960. Its tasks are to mark and to maintain the graves of members of the Commonwealth forces who were killed in the two world wars, to build memorials to those who have no known grave and to keep records and registers (including, after the Second World War, a record of civilian war dead).

There are graves in 140 different countries, and the Commission looks after 2,500 war cemeteries and smaller plots of ground. The cost of its work is shared by the governments of the United Kingdom, Canada, Australia, New Zealand, India, Pakistan and South Africa. Other Commonwealth countries contribute by bearing the cost of memorials in their own lands.

An instance of the literally endless nature of the Commission's work occurs in the *Sixty-Fourth Annual Report 1982–83*, which records the discovery on the Somme in France of sixty-one soldiers of the First World War – the largest such discovery for a good many years. Individual identification was impossible, but it was established that the remains came from five different British infantry regiments, and there were two Germans. The probability is that all these men were at an Advanced Dressing Station which was hit by gunfire. All of them have now had a permanent burial in the Commission's cemetery at Terlincthun.

Although the Commission's Charter relates only to the two world wars, the government turned to it in 1982 for assistance with the commemoration of those who died in the fighting on and around the Falkland Islands.

Anyone visiting the Western Front who wishes to trace a particular grave or cemetery should get in touch with:

The Commonwealth War Graves Commission
2 Marlow Road
Maidenhead
Berkshire
SL6 7DX
tel. 0628 34221

The staff are always helpful, courteous and infinitely patient, and cannot be praised too highly. The Commission also maintains an office in Ypres at 82 Elverdingestraat.

Finally, it is worth mentioning that the two largest memorials maintained by the Commission record the missing of two battles. The names on the Thiepval Memorial to the Missing of the Somme number 72,081; and on the Menin Gate Memorial to the Missing of the Ypres Salient, 54,360.

THE CEMETERIES

These are well signposted and never difficult to find. In every one there is a brass box decorated with a cross. In the larger cemeteries this is to be found in the shelter, and in the smaller ones it will be beside the wrought-iron entrance gates. Each box contains the Cemetery Register, which comprises a plan of the burial ground, a brief description of the origins of the burial and the fighting in the area, and an alphabetical list of the dead with personal details and instructions as to how to locate a particular grave. There is also a Visitors' Book.

Headstones are of uniform size, irrespective of rank. They stand about 2 ft 8 in. high and indicate, where known, name, rank, regiment, regimental crest, unit, date of death, age and religious emblem.

At the bottom is a space for an inscription chosen by the family. Foreign and enemy soldiers buried in Commission cemeteries usually have a white headstone of a slightly different shape. Repatriation of bodies is not permitted. Where bodies are un-identified the inscription reads: 'A Soldier of the Great War Known to God'. This was chosen by Rudyard Kipling, literary adviser to the Commission in 1919, who had himself lost a son on the Western Front.

The Poppy Legend

The link between the Great War and poppies is a strong one. This scarlet flower has come to sym-bolize the sacrifice of human life involved in war, together with remembrance of it.

On many Western Front battlefields where the land was laid waste, the ground was soon ablaze with poppies. Such symbolism proved irresistible to a Canadian war poet, John McCrae, and his poem 'In Flanders Fields' was originally published in *Punch* on 8 December 1915. The first of its three verses ran:

> In Flanders fields the poppies blow
> Between the crosses, row on row,
>   That mark our place; and in the sky
>   The larks, still bravely singing, fly
> Scarce heard amid the guns below.

Battlefield Debris

The vast expenditure of ammunition and equipment on the Western Front has left a potentially dangerous legacy for visitors. Farmers are constantly ploughing up rusted unexploded shells, bayonets and the like. In Belgium alone the military authorities are being called upon to deal with an average of 500 tons per year of such material.

All this represents a very real danger for the unwary traveller, who is well advised not to touch anything found *in situ*. There are plenty of places where 'safe' souvenirs may be purchased.

Demarcation Stones

A much depleted number of these stones – originally there were 119 of them – now remains. They were erected in Belgium and France in the decade following the Armistice to mark the limit of the German advance in 1918. The Touring Club of France and the Touring Club of Belgium initiated the scheme, and money flooded in to pay for the erection of these stones from local authorities, ex-servicemen's organizations and individual subscribers as well.

The stones, no more than one metre high, were carved in pink granite from a design by the sculptor Paul Moreau Vauthier. There were three main types, each characterized by a helmet of British, French or Belgian design which surmounted the monument. The sides of the stone were decorated with various

items of military equipment – water-bottle, res-
pirator case, etc. There was an inscription in English, French or Flemish on each stone, and this read:
'Here the Invader was brought to a standstill'.

Many of these memorials were lost or destroyed
during the Second World War, and the building of
motorways and other developments has meant the
disappearance of others. Of the seven originally
erected in the Ypres Salient, for instance, only two
or three have survived. One of them can be seen on
the Ypres to Wijtschate Road, near the canal, about
a mile north of St Eloois (Saint-Eloi) village.

Some Main Events
1914–1918

1914

28 June	Archduke Franz Ferdinand assassinated in Sarajevo.
1 August	Germany declares war on Russia.
2–3 August	German troops move into Belgium; as a consequence
4 August	Britain declares war on Germany.
23 August	Battle of Mons.
6 September	First Battle of the Marne begins.
19 October	First Battle of Ypres begins.
8 December	Admiral von Spee defeated at the Battle of the Falkland Islands.

1915

22 April	Second Battle of Ypres begins. Germans use poison gas.
25 April	Allied troops land on the Gallipoli Peninsula.
7 May	*Lusitania* torpedoed by a German U-boat.
16 June	Lloyd George becomes Minister for Munitions.
25 September	Battle of Loos begins.
19 December	Douglas Haig succeeds Sir John French as British Commander-in-Chief on the Western Front.

1916

8–9 January	Evacuation of the Gallipoli Peninsula by night.
21 February	Battle of Verdun begins.
1 July	Battle of the Somme begins.
29 August	Hindenburg becomes German Chief of Staff.

15 September	British tanks used for the first time (during the Battle of the Somme).
7 December	Lloyd George succeeds Asquith as Prime Minister.

1917

15 March	Czar of Russia abdicates.
6 April	USA declares war on Germany.
9 April	Battle of Arras begins.
6 July	Col. T. E. Lawrence ('Lawrence of Arabia'), with Arab forces, occupies Akaba.
31 July	Third Battle of Ypres begins.
20 November	Battle of Cambrai begins. Tanks used successfully for the first time.
9 December	Allenby enters Jerusalem.

1918

8 January	President Wilson of the USA puts forward a fourteen-point peace plan.
25 February	Food rationing introduced in Britain.
21 March	German offensive. British Army retreats, reducing the size of the Ypres Salient.
15 July	Second Battle of the Marne begins.
29 September	German line broken.
23 October	President Wilson demands the surrender of Germany.
28 October	Ludendorff, German Commander-in-Chief, resigns.
29 October	German sailors mutiny at Kiel.
9 November	The Kaiser abdicates.
11 November	General Armistice declared.
25 November	The only undefeated German Commander, General von Lettow-Vorbeck, surrenders at Abercorn in Northern Rhodesia (now Zambia).
	His force consisted of 155 Europeans, 4,275

Africans, 1 field gun, 24 Maxim machine-guns and 14 Lewis guns. The surrender was delayed because of communication difficulties – the German force was in the African bush.

Calais to Ypres

(via Saint-Omer)

Leave Calais on the N 43 and reach Saint-Omer in 40 km.

Saint-Omer

Set on hills between canals, this is a charming town that has a long history, both in its own right and in its contact with England. Hereward the Wake is said to have stayed here in Saxon times, and in the Middle Ages and in the early eighteenth century English soldiers were about.

During the Great War there was a considerable British presence; indeed, from October 1914 to March 1916 British General Headquarters was in Saint-Omer. In 1917 it was raided by enemy aircraft, and during the German spring offensive of 1918 it very soon – though fairly briefly – came within range of German artillery. There are few signs today that the British Army was ever here in large numbers, but there are points of interest.

A small, bluish plaque (similar to those put on to buildings of historic interest by the London County Council, and later the Greater London Council) on the wall of 50 avenue Carnot records the death in the house of Field Marshal Lord Roberts on 14 November 1914, after he developed pneumonia on a visit to the Indian Corps. Also in the Avenue Carnot is the Hôtel Sandelin, which is both a provincial museum and an art gallery. Number 37 rue Bertin was once the residence of Sir John French, and later of Sir Douglas Haig. Further down this street, which leads to the ruins of the Abbey of Saint-Bertin, are the buildings once used as a military hospital, and previous to that as a school for Roman Catholic boys from Britain, which was opened in 1592, moved later to Bruges, then Liège, in Belgium, and later still to Stonyhurst in Lancashire – where it is still flourishing. In the Jardin Public remains of the Vauban fortifications are preserved below the hill upon which the Basilica of Notre-Dame stands.

Leave Saint-Omer on the N 42 eastwards towards Hazebrouck, which is about 20 km. distant.

Hazebrouck

Once used as a major base by the Duke of Wellington's forces, Hazebrouck became a British headquarters town in October 1914, and over the next few years it developed into a large advanced base for the BEF. It was an important railway junction, and thousands of troops passed through its station on their way to Flanders or the battlefields of the Somme.

Towards the end of 1917 the town was damaged by enemy shellfire, but although it was threatened by the Germans during their 1918 spring offensive, and the civilian population was evacuated, Hazebrouck did not fall into their hands. Today there is little on its outskirts to remind us of the transport depots, hospitals and workshops that once stood here. The town itself was badly damaged in the Second World War, but, since the older buildings have been repaired in their period style, Hazebrouck, around its huge marketplace, does look rather as it appeared when the BEF was here – and in a few places cobblestones have survived!

Leave Hazebrouck by the N 42, the Rue de Bailleul, which passes through the area of fighting around the town of April 1918. The village of Strazeele, 7 km. away, was the first enemy objective, but the Australians held back their advance while the villages of Méteren and Merris to the north-east and south respectively were overrun by the Germans, and not retaken until the early days of July. Four kilometres further on, the N 42 crosses the Dunkerque–Lille motorway; and in 3 km., now on the D 944, you come into Bailleul.

Bailleul

A base town, Bailleul was almost in the front line for much of the war. The Germans occupied it briefly in 1914, but by mid-October it was in British hands and remained so for the next three and a half years. In July 1917 enemy artillery fire caused considerable damage. Then, in April 1918, the Germans advanced into Bailleul, and not until August were its ruins retaken by the British 25th Division.

As you come into the centre of the town there is a roundabout, in the middle of which is the 25th Division memorial. Turn left and enter the central square. In one of the streets behind this are the ruins of Saint-Amand Church, which form an integral part of the town war memorial.

Leave for Belgium on the D 23 at the opposite end of the square. Almost immediately you will see a CWGC sign indicating, to the right down a small street, the way to the Bailleul Communal Cemetery and Extension, where over 4,000 men of many nationalities are buried.

Stay on (or return to) the D 23 and arrive at the Belgian frontier in some 4 km. Take the N 375 for Ypres (Ieper), and about 5 km. further on there is a wooded slope on the right of the road with remains of a trench system just visible above the treeline. This is the Scherpenberg, which was successfully defended by French and British troops when the Germans attacked it at the end of April 1918. A photograph of it taken after the fighting and published in the Michelin Guide *Ypres and the Battles of Ypres* (1919) shows an area of utter devastation, with debris, including sheets of corrugated iron, scattered over the hill. Trees, where they had survived, were just trunks with stunted branches. Such a scene compares almost unbearably with today's calm, and underlines the difficulty for the modern traveller of imagining the landscape as it was then.

In a cottage on Scherpenberg lived two old women – the younger of the two was about eighty years old – who were the only civilians not to have been evacuated from the fighting zone. It was only with the greatest difficulty that an unknown officer serving with a Divisional Ammunition Column persuaded them to leave their home and seek shelter in Poperinge. Leaving the cottage where they had lived since birth was more terrifying to them than continuing to endure the German shells which had well-nigh destroyed it. But go they did, tramping along the country road towards Poperinge, clutching pathetic bundles containing the only possessions left to them. It is not known whether they ever returned . . .[19]

Continue about 10 km. into Ypres.

The Three Battles
of Ypres

First Ypres
19 October 1914 to 22 November 1914

In mid-October British troops moving northwards
through Ypres dislodged the Germans who had
briefly occupied the town, and drove them back to
the Passchendaele Ridge. At about the same time,
repeated attempts were being made by the Germans
to break through the Allied line and reach the
Channel ports. This initial assault was beaten off,
with heavy casualties on both sides. Then, on 29
October, the enemy launched a new offensive with
an attack between Messines and Geluveld, and this
was followed up in November with a new attack on
the front which ran from Comines to Dixmuide.
Despite even more appalling casualties the results of
the fighting were inconclusive, and it petered out.
As it did so, both sides began to dig in; and
when the Belgians flooded the low-lying land from
Dixmuide to the sea, there was a battle zone
or front line which ran from the North Sea to
the Swiss frontier. The Western Front had been
born.

Casualties:

British	58,000
French	50,000
German	130,000

Second Ypres
22 April 1915 to 25 May 1915

Late in the afternoon of 22 April, in the area of Poelkapelle, Langemark and Bikschote, as the prelude to an attack on the Ypres front, the Germans released poison gas. French colonial troops took the brunt of this assault and, fearful of the menacing cloud moving towards them, broke and ran for their lives. The Germans, however, did not intend to capture the town. Their aim was much more limited: to take Pilkem Ridge. By the time darkness fell it was in their hands and they began to dig in. It was only on the following morning, in the full light of day, that the German commander could see the extraordinary impact that the gas attack had made. Had the onset been pressed, it is likely that Ypres would have fallen and the road to the Channel ports would have been open.

The Allies reacted to the threat overnight. Troops from the 1st Canadian Division were hastily regrouped to fill the gap in the line left by the unceremonious retreat of the French colonial troops, and in conjunction with the Northumbrian Division they began a series of holding actions and counter-attacks. On 24 April, between St Juliaan and Passchendaele, the Germans launched a second gas

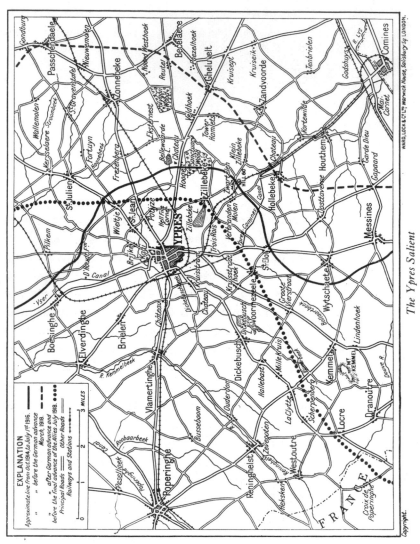

The Ypres Salient

attack. With gas-masks improvised from hand-kerchiefs or similar material soaked in water, the British line – despite heavy casualties – held; but the initial gains made by the enemy were so considerable that it was deemed necessary for the British to shorten their defence line, and they did so on 2

May. Over the following three weeks the battle petered out, leaving the Germans occupying both Pilkem Ridge and the high ground bordering the southern end of the Salient.

Casualties:

British	60,000
French	10,000
German	35,000

Third Ypres
31 July 1917 to 10 November 1917

In April 1917 things were going badly for the French. General Nivelle, who had achieved fame at Verdun in the previous year, initiated the Battle of the Aisne. Before it began he had let it be known – even to the enemy, for his security was bad – that he would drive the invader from French soil. In the event, after a series of disastrous engagements, he signally failed to do so. His casualty lists were enormously long, and many French soldiers were provoked to mutiny. Over 20,000 mutineers were tried by courts martial; fifty-five of them were shot, and there were lesser punishments for many others who stood trial. The French government was badly shaken, and Marshal Joffre went to the United States to seek reassurance that an American declaration of war would be speedily followed by the appearance in France of an expeditionary force ready to fight side by side with the Allied forces. Had such an assurance not been received, it is possible that France might have sued for a separate peace with Germany. In an atmosphere of shock and heavy with uncertainty, General Pétain – later Marshal Pétain, head of the Vichy government in France during the Second World War – began to rebuild the shattered morale of the French army; and it was apparent that he would need a breathing space if he were to do so successfully. This meant taking as much pressure as possible off French soldiers holding front-line trenches, and after consultation with the British Commander-in-Chief, General Haig, it was decided that British troops should divert German attention away from the French line.

Haig's motives in agreeing to assist the French in this way were inevitably mixed. On the one hand, he was under some pressure from the British war cabinet, led by Lloyd George, to avoid unnecessary casualties – but equally there was the chance that a skilful victory over the Germans in Flanders would vindicate his own aggressive policies of keeping up pressure on the enemy, policies which had led to long casualty lists with little to show for them in terms of any major advance, and which were causing increasing concern at home. And, of course, what Haig wanted, at almost any cost, was a British victory over the German army before the arrival of significant numbers of American troops in Europe.

So the Third Battle of Ypres began. It was, in fact, two battles. First there was the Battle of Messines. Ever since the British withdrawal in 1915 at Second Ypres, the Germans had occupied all the high ground at the southern edge of the Salient. The Messines–Wytschaete (Mesen–Wijtschate) Ridge was of especial value to the Germans because from it they could cover much of the British trench system

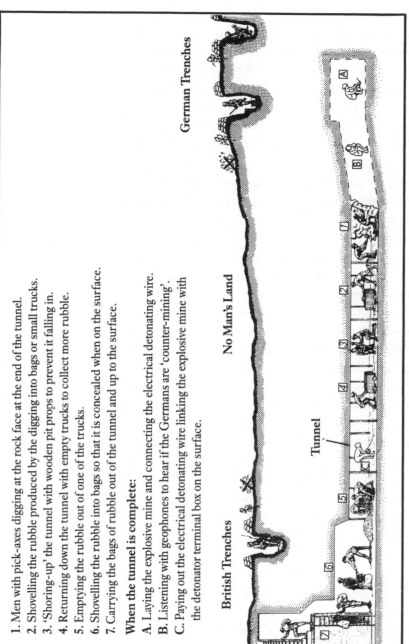

1. Men with pick-axes digging at the rock face at the end of the tunnel.
2. Shovelling the rubble produced by the digging into bags or small trucks.
3. 'Shoring-up' the tunnel with wooden pit props to prevent it falling in.
4. Returning down the tunnel with empty trucks to collect more rubble.
5. Emptying the rubble out of one of the trucks.
6. Shovelling the rubble into bags so that it is concealed when on the surface.
7. Carrying the bags of rubble out of the tunnel and up to the surface.

When the tunnel is complete:

A. Laying the explosive mine and connecting the electrical detonating wire.
B. Listening with geophones to hear if the Germans are 'counter-mining'.
C. Paying out the electrical detonating wire linking the explosive mine with the detonator terminal box on the surface.

German Trenches

No Man's Land

Tunnel

British Trenches

Tunnelling and laying mines

with enfilade fire, and during the hours of daylight
they could observe the supply route which ran from
Poperinge via Vlamertinge to Ypres. The British
Second Army, commanded by General Plumer –
sometimes known as 'the Warden of the Salient' –
was given the task of driving the Germans off the
Ridge. On 7 June, at ten minutes past three in the
morning, nineteen mines that had previously been
put into position by tunnelling companies, working
with consummate skill and at great risk to themselves
beneath the German lines, were exploded. The noise
was tremendous – some said it was heard in south-
eastern England. The effect upon the Germans was
staggering . . . and taking advantage of the shock
effect upon the enemy, the Second Army, supported
by more than 2,000 heavy guns and poison gas,
moved forward. Almost the entire Ridge was taken
that day. The attack was a complete success.

Not so the second phase, which was an attack
upon the Gheluvelt–Passchendaele (Geluveld–
Passendale) Ridge with the aim of piercing the
German line and breaking through to the North Sea
coast. It was an ambitious plan, and responsibility
for it was given to the Fifth Army, commanded by
General Gough. More than 3,000 guns took part in
the preliminary ten-day bombardment; then on 31
July the twelve divisions of Gough's army went into
action. Persistent heavy rain and the destruction of
the drainage system of the low-lying plains by
repeated heavy bombardment meant that the ground
over which the attackers were attempting to press
forward became a quagmire; but Haig persisted with
the assault. Gough, the army commander, recommended that the battle should be broken off.
Haig insisted upon its continuance. New attacks

were repeatedly launched, the rain did not stop and the mud – to say nothing of enemy fire – claimed more and more victims. Eventually, on 6 November, more than three months after the battle had begun, Passchendaele village was taken. Four days later, on the 10th, the Ridge was secured, and Third Ypres ended. The British army suffered 300,000 casualties. Thirty-five men had died for every metre of ground wrested from the enemy.

Casualties:

British   300,000
French   8,500
German   260,000

During the three battles of Ypres a total of eighty-four Victoria Crosses were awarded for acts of extreme gallantry in the field.

Ypres

The origins of the town of Ypres are uncertain. Word has it that a British chief settled in the neighbourhood with some seven hundred German slaves in about AD 960. The Latin form of his name was *Hypra*, and the settlement was named after him. By the twelfth century there was a population of 20,000, and there were seven churches. At this period in the Middle Ages Ypres was most famous for the cloth produced by its weavers. The most imposing building in the town was the Cloth Hall in the Market Square (Grote Markt in Flemish,

Grande Place in French). It was constructed over a very long period indeed, and was not completed until 1624.

Ypres has had a very chequered history. At one time its population grew to 40,000, but, because of its strategic position *vis-à-vis* the roads and waterways of Flanders, the area surrounding it was the scene of much fighting between various armies and the town itself was several times besieged. A plague in 1584 laid waste the population, which dwindled to around 5,000. This disaster was followed by a series of military occupations: at one time or another French, Austrian, Dutch and Spanish troops held the town. It was, however, the French who left the most permanent mark upon it, because the military architect Vauban supervised the design and building of the ramparts erected to pro-tect it.

Eventually agriculture began to supplant weaving and cloth-making as the main source of the town's wealth, and besides being a considerable market for hops, beetroot, chicory and corn, Ypres became an important butter market. In the Cloth Hall there was a large chamber called the Butter Hall, and near by there is Boterstraat (Butter Street).

When the Great War broke out in 1914 Ypres was an obscure, but still prosperous, town. Few people outside Belgium had ever heard of it. Its prosperity, however, was soon to be shattered. Be-cause of its position on the Flanders plain, standing amid a complex of small waterways whose function it was to keep the soil drained, its strategic im-portance between 1914 and 1918 was as great as it had been in earlier conflicts. For three days in October 1914 the town was occupied by German

troops. They were pushed out by the British, and
the Germans then took up positions on the low-
lying ridges facing the town which ran in a rough
half-circle from Passchendaele in the north-east
round to Messines and Kemmel, which lay to the
south. It was from this ridge that the enemy, well
dug in, were able to overlook the British positions.

The battles of autumn and winter 1914 were
bloody though indecisive, and after them both sides
attempted to outflank each other in a 'race to the
sea'. The result was a line of opposing trenches
which ran from somewhere beyond Nieuwpoort on
the Belgian coast down to the Swiss frontier in the
south. From their trenches each side faced the other
in what was to become, in many sectors, a war of bitter and unceasing attrition, where the long casualty
lists bore no relationship at all to the advantages
gained by attack. Trench warfare was essentially
static. In front of Ypres the British line, following

*The Menin Gate
as it was known to
the B E F*

the First Battle of Ypres, bulged into the German line – and so the 'Salient' was born. It was the scene of some of the most hard-fought battles of the entire war, and was regarded by both sides as a crucial point. The British army, on the one hand, made repeated attempts to fight its way on to the ridges and beyond, while the Germans wanted to reoccupy the town and push on to the Channel ports. Fighting was continuous, erupting on three occasions into major battles. The town itself was reduced to rubble – by 1918 a soldier on horseback could see from one end of it to the other . . . The jagged ruins of the Cloth Hall were virtually the only reminder of the once-thriving town.

There are very nearly 600 military cemeteries looked after by the Commonwealth War Graves Commission in the Salient. Almost a quarter of a million men of the British and Commonwealth armies are buried there. Nearly 100,000 have no known grave, and their names are recorded on the Menin Gate, through which so many soldiers passed on their way to the front line, at Tyne Cot Cemetery and on the Ploegsteert Memorial.

The small area of ground covered by the Salient gives an added poignancy to the casualty figures. Why was it held with such tenacity? When General Sir Horace Smith-Dorrien proposed, in 1915, to reduce its size, he was promptly sacked. In 1918, after the final German offensive, the British were forced to withdraw and the army held a much reduced area that consisted, in effect, of nothing much more than Ypres and its outskirts. This was virtually the line that Smith-Dorrien had suggested four years or so earlier. The extraordinary courage of the fighting soldiers and their support services is not in question; but the wisdom of the Commander-in-Chief, particularly in regard to the Third Battle of Ypres, when the ground fought over had been reduced to a quagmire and repeated attacks were ordered, must be called into question.

AN YPRES CALENDAR

Ypres (usually known to the BEF as 'Wipers' or 'Eepree') attracts a large number of visitors each year, and a high proportion of them have an interest in the war of 1914–18. Since the town is now twinned with Sittingbourne in Kent, some activities are arranged jointly.

The major annual events are these:

Second Sunday in May	Annual Festival of the Cats A colourful carnival with toy cats – they were live ones in the Middle Ages! – being thrown from the Cloth Hall belfry.
Weekend after Ascension	100 Kilometres of Ypres March
Last weekend in June	24 Hours of Ypres Automobile Rally
Last Sunday in August	4 Days of the Yser March
Second weekend in September	The *Tooghedagen* This is a craft and antiques fair.
10 November	Procession of St Martin
11 November	Armistice Day Unlike the practice now in Britain, the Armistice is always celebrated on this date, no matter what day it falls upon.

The highlight of any visit to the battlefields must surely be to witness the playing of the Last Post at the Menin Gate (Menenpoort). It is usually sounded by two buglers from the Fire Brigade, although more take part on special anniversaries, and the simple ceremony takes place *every evening of the year* at 8 p.m. (20.00), whatever the weather, with the police holding up the traffic. It is a deeply moving event, and its poignancy does not in any sense diminish with the passing years.

Within a recess of the Gate there is a Visitors' Book, which may be signed, and if groups or individuals wish to lay wreaths under one of the side arches a special ceremony can be arranged by the Last Post Committee. They can be contacted through the Ypres Tourist Office in the Cloth Hall, and there they will, if you wish, also put you in touch with the Royal British Legion, Ypres Branch.

The Menin Gate, a Memorial to the Missing in the Salient, is the most impressive edifice for the British or Commonwealth visitor to see in the town. It is an archway straddling the road, designed by Sir Reginald Blomfield and inaugurated on 24 July 1927 by Field Marshal Plumer, who had commanded troops defending Ypres for much of the war. Carved upon it are 54,896 names.

Long before the outbreak of hostilities in 1914 the original town gate had disappeared and its site was marked by two stone lions, one on each side of the road. These are now in Canberra, Australia – a tangible reminder of the part played by that country's soldiers on the Western Front. It was along this road that thousands of men tramped on their way to the line; but because this exit was so exposed to German shellfire the Lille Gate (Rijselpoort), which lies to the south of Ypres, became the main exit for troops leaving the town *en route* for the trenches. In no way, however, is the importance of the Menin Gate Memorial and the Last Post Ceremony lessened on this account.

The idea for the ceremony came from the then superintendent of police, M. P. Vandenbraambussche, and the practice of playing the Last Post every evening began in the early summer of 1928, nearly a year after the inauguration of the memorial. It was discontinued in October of that year, but restarted on 11 November 1929. With the exception of a break during the German occupation of Ypres (20 May 1940 to 6 September 1944), it has continued ever since – and it is perhaps worth recalling that, on the day the Germans left the town, Last Post was played at the Menin Gate that evening.

Finally, it should be said that the ramparts which still encircle the eastern and southern sectors of the town provide an interesting walk. The stretch of wall adjoining the Lille Gate has been left just as it was in 1918. Below and within it British troops found shelter from the bombardments which laid waste the town. Just across from the Gate is Ramparts Cemetery, the only British military burial place within the old walls of the town.

See Ypres, Itinerary 3, p. 124.

The Ypres Battlefields

The visitor who wants to look at this area in some detail is advised to follow three itineraries. It must, however, be stressed that these in no way correspond to the three battles of Ypres. The area is too small, and the fighting too concentrated. For the dyed-in-the-wool military enthusiast, three months would probably not be too long a period in which to explore the Salient, but the majority of travellers will not want to spend more than a day or two. If only one day is possible, itinerary 1 should be followed; itineraries 2 and 3 on successive days if time permits.

ITINERARY 1

The best place to start a tour of the Salient is in Ypres itself. Park in the Grote Markt (Market Square).* Then, stand in roughly the middle of the square, imagining yourself at the centre of a clock face, with the Cloth Hall as you face it at twelve o'clock. Slightly to the right, at one o'clock, is Diksmuidestraat, the road leading to Bruges (Brugge). To the right, at four o'clock, is the road that leads to the Menin Gate. And behind you, at seven o'clock, is the Rijselstraat, which leads to the Lille Gate. At ten o'clock is the road to Poperinge.

Tourist Office
You will find this in the Cloth Hall under the vaulted covered walkway. Open 08.00–12.15 and 14.00–17.15 Tuesday, Wednesday, Thursday and Friday; closed on Monday and Saturday afternoons and all day Sunday. Maps, books, postcards and tourist information are available. English is spoken. It is worth buying here the Westoek Flanders Tourist Map, 1:132,000. This gives quite the best repre-

---

* On Saturdays there is a busy market in the square and parking is difficult until an hour or so after midday.

sentation of the topography of the Salient. Heights and woods are indicated in colour.

Salient Museum

This is next door to the Tourist Office. At its entrance are two Second World War sea mines, but exhibits are all concerned with the Great War. There is a small entrance fee, and the museum is open every day 09.30–12.15 and 13.30–17.30 from 1 April to 31 October. At other times of the year it is open on Sundays only 10.00–12.00 and 14.00–18.00. As you leave the museum, turn left, through the archway, keep left and find the entrance to the cathedral.

St Martin's Cathedral

The building of the cathedral was begun in 1221. Completely destroyed during the Great War, it has been rebuilt to the original plans, including the 100 m. Gothic spire which the town was unable to afford in 1421! There is a statue of Notre-Dame of Thuyne, Patroness of Ypres, and over the south door there is a rose window which is the British Memorial to King Albert of the Belgians. Turn right out of the main door and cross the road. It is about 100 m. to the corner of Elvedingestraat, and round the corner on the left is the entrance to a church.

St George's Memorial Church

On 24 July 1927 Field Marshal Lord Plumer laid the foundation stone of this church, for the building of which Field Marshal Sir John French had made an appeal in 1924. It was dedicated on 24 March 1929, and is a memorial to the British presence in Ypres and in the Salient during the Great War.

Practically every item in it is a memorial to an individual or a regiment. During the Second World War, while Ypres was occupied by the Germans, the stained glass in the church was removed for safety, and it was replaced in 1947. Other more portable items were looked after by individuals in the town . . . Such action symbolizes the close connection between local people and the church, which still serves the local community.

Return towards the cathedral, but continue along J. Coomensstraat to the T-junction. On the right you will see the Belgian War Memorial, which is to the dead of both world wars. The Cloth Hall is on the left; turn along its side and opposite the Lille (Rijsel) exit, set into the wall, there is a small French Memorial plaque.

From the car park you can see the Regina Hotel with its Old Bill Pub sign.* The Tea Room at No. 9 is of interest as the first building in the square to be rebuilt. The new section of Cloth Hall (Nieuwwerck) is built in Spanish Renaissance style – a vivid

---

* 'Old Bill' was an archetypal old soldier created by Captain Bruce Bairnsfather in a series of cartoons published in a weekly magazine called *The Bystander*, and later published in separate collections. Characterized by a walrus moustache, 'Old Bill' possessed a resilience and cockney humour that made him a survivor. Among the best-known cartoons is one showing him sitting outside a flooded dug-out. To a passing soldier he says: 'Why carn't yer find a place for yourself and keep yer — feet out of the water I got to sleep in?' He also figured on a recruiting poster for the Territorial Army drawn by Bairnsfather at the end of 1938. It showed a much aged, though still recognizable, 'Old Bill' pointing to an armoured fighting vehicle and saying to a young man: 'Yes, son, that's what I'd be doing, if I 'ad my time over again!' The legend at the base of the poster proclaims: 'And Old Bill ought to know.'

Bairnsfather wrote about his wartime experiences in *Bullets and Billets*, published, with many illustrations, in 1916. His autobiography, *Wide Canvas*, appeared in 1939.

'Look out, Bill, you're sittin' on a wasps' nest'

THE COMMUNICATION TRENCH

PROBLEM – *whether to walk along the top and risk it, or do another mile of this*

reminder of the Spanish occupation in the sixteenth century.

From the Grote Markt take the Diksmuidestraat exit and follow the signs for Brugge. Cross over the traffic lights after about 1 km., and follow the N 313 and signs to Roeselare and Poelkapelle. The road soon crosses Bellewaerdebeek and begins to rise as you come to the village of St Jan. Whitehouse Cemetery can be seen on the left. This was commenced in March 1916, and many bodies were added after the Armistice. There are 1,145 graves here.

Continue on the N 313 to St Jan.

St Jan

During the Second Battle of Ypres in 1915 the village was largely destroyed by German artillery fire. The Canadians, who were fighting about 2 km. from St Jan, used the area for casualty clearing stations, which were mostly situated in cellars. Prisoners of war were assembled here as well.

Continue on the N 313. Driving roughly north-east you are travelling towards the German lines.

Wieltje Farm and Oxford Road cemeteries

After ½ km. take the right fork for Wieltje Farm Cemetery, where 115 graves are recorded, mostly from the fighting of July to October 1917 (Third Battle of Ypres). The road forward from here was known to the troops as Paradise Alley. On the right is Oxford Road Cemetery, and beyond the lane on the right is the 59th Northumbrian Divisional Memorial, which has a later inscription upon it relating to the Second World War. In the fields behind the memorial there were two lines of bunkers and emplacements, which are now, for the most part, barely visible above the ground, but they mark the line of the Cambrai Redoubt of 1917.

Come back to the N 313. Ahead of you is the new motorway bridge, and to the right the village of Wieltje.

Wieltje

This small village was the site of a large ammunition dump in 1915 before the Second Battle of Ypres. In 1917 the German line ran across the N 313 at this point. A German pillbox can be seen in the field between the village and the motorway – during the construction of which three others in the vicinity were destroyed. The defences in this area were called Cambrai Lane, Cambrai Trench, Call Trench and Call Support. The village changed hands several times during the war.

Continue under the bridge to the junction with the new by-pass road. To the right is a yellow sign for St Juliaan, and on the left at about 200 m. a group of buildings represent Mousetrap Farm.

Mousetrap Farm
The buildings you can see were, in fact, put up in
1920 about 200 m. further south than the originals,
which were destroyed in the fighting. The Germans
called it Wieltje Château, the French and Belgians
Château du Nord, while to the British it was Shell
Trap Farm. Since this name was considered too
ominous it was officially changed by Corps Headquarters to Mousetrap Farm, which was felt to be
rather less intimidating. During April 1915 the 3rd
Canadian Brigade used it as a headquarters; after
the gas attack of 1915 it became part of the front
line, and the German advance was stopped at this
point by Canadian troops.

Turn right in the direction of Poelkapelle and
Lichtervelde on the N 313. Immediately to your left
you will see the Seaforths Cemetery, named after
the Seaforth Highlanders, whose dead make up the
majority of the burials. Beside the cemetery are some
farm buildings on the site of Cheddar Villa.

Cheddar Villa
The Canadians held this area before the Second
Battle of Ypres in 1915, but it was captured by the
Germans following the gas attack and a large concrete blockhouse was constructed. On the opening
day of the Third Battle of Ypres in 1917, this was
captured by the British and used as a Regimental
Aid Post. Since it had started life as a German fortification with an entrance facing their rear, it now
faced the British front; and a week later a German
shell burst near the entrance causing deaths and
casualties to a platoon of the 1st Buckinghamshires
sheltering inside it.

Part of this old German blockhouse has been

incorporated into the farm outbuildings. Somewhere between Cheddar Villa and the next village, St Juliaan, Bruce Bairnsfather (see footnote, p. 88) was wounded on 25 April 1915. Six hundred metres further on, the road crosses at a right angle the German line where a row of pillboxes stood. They ran roughly from the Steenbeek stream on the right, westwards for 1½ km. to Kitchener's Wood, now an open field. They formed, with a supporting trench system, a very formidable defensive line, which was known to the British army fighting there as 'Canteen' to the east of the road and 'Canopus' and 'Canoe' to the right.

Continue to St Juliaan village and turn left up a small road (Pepperstraat) beside a telephone exchange tower and a bus stop. Stop after about 150 m. beyond the houses on the right.

St Juliaan German Bunker

To the right, about 100 m. away, you can see a large German bunker that formed part of the Alberta defences during the Third Battle of Ypres in 1917. It was eventually captured by men of the 16th Battalion Sherwood Foresters during this battle.

Return to the N 313, turn left and continue through the village.

St Juliaan

This was captured by the Germans on 24 April 1915, the first day of the second gas attack. They then set about building its concrete defences, and it was retaken by the British 29th Division in the early days of Third Ypres. The area of the first gas attack is roughly covered by the road from St Juliaan to just short of Poelkapelle, and the ground would have been covered on 22 April 1915 with greenish-yellow chlorine. Continue to the St Juliaan Monument sign and crossroads. Turn right at the sign to Zonnebeke and park on the left.

Vancouver Corner. Brooding Soldier

This monument commemorates the 18,000 Canadian soldiers who faced the enemy after the Germans' first gas attacks on 22–24 April 1915 . . . 2,000 of them were killed. The monument, carved from a single shaft of granite by Chapman Clemesha, himself wounded during the war, was unveiled by the Duke of Connaught on 8 July 1923. Notice that the cedars surrounding it are trimmed to represent the shape of shells.

Continue 100 m. towards Zonnebeke and take the small road to the left, Vrouwstraat, signposted 'ROUTE '14–18'. This leads to Death Mill.

Death Mill (Totenmühle)

The Germans used the original mill on this site as an observation post. The Flanders countryside is so flat that even a few metres' extra height would give greatly increased visibility and enable artillery observation officers to direct the fire of their guns.

Continue to the right of the mill, and the route to Tyne Cot (see below) is clearly indicated by white 'ROUTE '14–18' markers. Pass a small junction on the left, and stop at the next junction to the right, opposite a calvary.

At this point you are pretty well in the centre of the battlefields of 1915 and 1917. Imagine that you are standing at the centre of a clockface and 12 o'clock represents the direction in which you are travelling. Ahead of you, running from 11 o'clock to

2 o'clock, is the Passchendaele–Messines Ridge, culminating just beyond 2 o'clock in the bulk of Kemmel Hill. At 10 o'clock the water tower of Passchendaele village is easily recognizable because of its rectangular shape, and at 11 o'clock is the spire of Passchendaele Church. Past the mill, at 6 o'clock, Langemark Church can be seen. Ypres is at 3 o'clock. At 11 o'clock it is possible, on a clear day, to make out a group of four poplar trees beyond the buildings on the near horizon. They mark Tyne Cot Cemetery. At the beginning of the Third Battle of Ypres in 1917 the German front line was at Cheddar Villa, and the spot where you are standing marks a point just behind the third German trench line. It took British and Commonwealth forces two and a half months to fight their way here from the Wieltje Farm area.

Continue along the road to the crossroads.

Crossroads. New Zealand Memorial
This column commemorates the men of the New Zealand Division who captured this area during the Battle of Broodseinde in April 1917. Continue over the crossroads on to Schipstraat, and Tyne Cot Cemetery is visible ahead – follow 'ROUTE '14–18' signs to it.

Tyne Cot Cemetery
This is the largest British war cemetery, containing about 12,000 graves and with a memorial to the 35,000 or so men who are recorded as missing and have no known grave. Entry is obtained through a flintstone lich-gate, and the view up a gentle slope to the Great Cross and Memorial to the Missing is deeply moving.

Three hundred and fifty graves were made during the war, and the remainder of the dead were brought here from the surrounding battlefields. Tyne Cot, designed by Herbert Baker, stands as a memorial to the British and Commonwealth armies that fought in the Ypres Salient. With its vast curving wall, terminating in domed pavilions punctuated by colonnaded recesses, it remains a moving tribute to the casualties of war.

The cemetery was so named by men of the 50th Northumbrian Division who were amongst the thousands of troops in this area. The German defences were a complex of heavily fortified bunkers and pillboxes. One of the pillboxes was used as an advanced dressing station after its capture, and at the suggestion of King George V the Cross of Sacrifice, which is the focal point of the cemetery, was built over a part of it. Today you can see a small part of this fortification below the cross.

Some seventy years after the war it is difficult, on looking back from the quiet of Tyne Cot across a peaceful landscape towards Ypres, to imagine the devastation of the land, the constant rain of autumn 1917 and the all-pervasive mud, to say nothing of the dogged endurance of the soldiers. Private F. Hodgson, a stretcher-bearer with the 11th Canadian Field Ambulance, recalled that 'it took six of us at a time to get one stretcher out through the mud . . . It was a terrible job carrying in the dark — almost impossible.'[20]

When you leave the cemetery, turn round and drive back along the road that skirts it. This is a gentle uphill drive along Tynecotstraat to the junction with Passchendaele. Turn left and continue to the church, which has some fine stained-glass windows commemorating St George and various Lancastrian units that served in the area. From the church there are signs leading to the Canadian Memorial. Return to Passchendaele and follow signs for Broodseinde and Beselare on the N 303, following Wervikstraat over the motorway towards the Menen Road. Turn right at Geluveld crossroads on to the N 8 back to Ypres.

Geluveld Crossroads

To the right is a windmill at the foot of which is a memorial to the 1st Battalion South Wales Borderers who, together with the 2nd Battalion Worcestershire Regiment, successfully counter-attacked a German advance in this area on 31 October 1914 during the First Battle of Ypres.

Continue – the road goes downhill, then rises to a crest and a road junction.

Clapham Junction

Several roads and tracks met at this point: hence the name given to it by soldiers. During the First Battle of Ypres in 1914 the 1st Battalion of the Gloucestershire Regiment was heavily engaged in the fighting here. In the following year, during Second Ypres, the 2nd Battalion of the Gloucesters was here. The memorial to both battalions is on the right; and opposite, on the left, is a similar one for the 18th (Eastern) Division.

The Gloucestershire Regiment was typical of the many county regiments which formed the backbone of the army and provided the base upon which wartime expansion took place. It was formed in 1881 by the amalgamation of the 28th (North Gloucestershire) Regiment and the 61st (South

Gloucestershire) Regiment, which became the 1st and 2nd Battalions respectively. The history and traditions of the regiment were, however, very much older than this date would suggest, for one or other – sometimes both – of the numbered regiments (established in 1694 and 1756) had taken part in Marlborough's campaigns and served in India, North America, Spain and Portugal, the Crimea, South Africa and elsewhere.

The Gloucesters had the unique distinction of wearing a badge at the back of their head-dress as well as at the front – in commemoration of the Battle of Alexandria (1801), when the regiment, attacked in the front and the rear, fought back to back. The privilege of wearing two badges was confirmed in 1830. For some recruits during the Second World War this proved a mixed blessing. Back-badges were all too easily lost, and the present writer remembers men at the regimental depot being turned back at the gate when they were about to leave barracks after duty because they had no back-badges and were 'improperly dressed' without them!

During the Great War the Gloucesters fought in all the major campaigns on the Western Front, and some of them served at Gallipoli and in Mesopotamia. They had an equally distinguished record in the Second World War, and during the Korean conflict the 1st Battalion was awarded the United States Presidential Citation in recognition of its service. It is one of the few infantry regiments in the army to have escaped the amalgamations that have taken place in recent years.

Continue on this road as it goes downhill past a leisure park on the right.

Hooge Château and Crater Cemetery

The leisure park covers roughly the area of Hooge Château, the destruction of which by shellfire began in the autumn of 1914. Two hundred metres further on the left is Crater Cemetery, begun during Third Ypres, where 5,892 graves are recorded; and facing it, by the church up Bellewaerdestraat, in a privately owned wood, is the crater that gives the cemetery its name. Created by a mine exploded by the 3rd Division, it is now a pond. It was in this area that the Germans first used flamethrowers in July 1915.

Continue down the hill for 500 m., then turn left up Canadalaan, by the 'Canada Café', to Sanctuary Wood.

Sanctuary Wood

There is a privately owned museum here, open all the year during daylight hours. Trenches, underground bunkers, battle artefacts and weapons can be seen, there are souvenirs and books for sale, and there is a café offering drinks and snacks. The cemetery close by contains the grave of Gilbert Talbot, after whom Toc H was named (see p. 122); and 300 m. further to the south is the Canadian Memorial at Hill 62.

Return down Canadalaan to the Menen Road. Turn left, and on your immediate left is another museum.

Menen Road Museum

This is a small museum, privately owned, with artefacts, uniforms and photographs.

Continue towards Ypres for 150 m., then take the first right along a small metalled road called Begijnenbosstraat. Follow signs to the Royal Engineers Grave.

THE INTELLIGENCE DEPARTMENT

"Is this 'ere the Warwicks?"
"Nao. 'Indenburg's blinkin' Light Infantry"

RE Grave. Railway Wood

An officer and eleven other ranks of the 177th (Tunnelling) Company Royal Engineers are buried here. For nearly two years the British front line trenches ran through this area, and many craters remain.

Return to Begijnenbosstraat, turn right, and at the T-junction with the main road turn right towards Zonnebeke. Immediately to your right there is a French military cemetery.

French National Cemetery.
Saint-Charles-Potijze

There are 3,748 graves here, and an *ossuaire* (mass grave) for 600 unknown soldiers. Continue towards Zonnebeke for ½ km. to Aeroplane Cemetery.

Aeroplane Cemetery

This is so called on account of a crashed aeroplane that was preserved for some years in front of the Cross. There are 1,097 graves here. Until Third Ypres this area was part of no-man's land, lying between the opposing front-line trenches.

Continue over the motorway, noting the three tall chimneys of the Terca Brickworks on your left. After the sign for Zonnebeke, cross the line of the old railway where the road bends left, turn right on the bend, and follow the signs to Polygon Wood, then 'ROUTE '14–18' along Lange Dreve.

Polygon Wood

On the right is a small cemetery containing 100 graves, mostly New Zealanders'; to the left is a re-planted Polygon Wood. The original was destroyed during the fighting, when the area changed hands no fewer than six times. The 5th Australian Memorial is on a mound that used to be part of an army training ground in use before 1870. Where the rifle ranges were is now the Buttes New British Cemetery, made after the Armistice and containing 2,066 graves.

Continue along Lange Dreve to the T-junction, turn left along Lotegatstraat, and follow the 'ROUTE '14-18' signs over the motorway and along Waterstraat to the junction with the Menen Road. Turn left towards Geluveld. Before you reach the windmill, turn right towards Zandvoorde.

Zandvoorde British Cemetery
As the road rises to the village you can see the cemetery off the road on your left. Over 1,500 burials are recorded, and bodies were brought here after the Armistice from temporary burials in the surrounding area. Continue to the T-junction, turn right on to Zillebekestraat and follow it through the village. Look out for, and take, a sharp bend to the left. This neighbourhood was the scene of fierce fighting in 1914 during First Ypres, and at the southern edge of the village is the Household Cavalry Memorial.

Continue towards Zillebeke, turn left in the village just after the houses begin, and follow signs to Hill 60. Park there at the Queen Victoria Rifles Café.

Hill 60
Named after its height above sea level, this is an artificial hill made from spoil taken from the railway cutting some 100 m. to the south. It was heavily fought over and changed hands several times. A

good deal of tunnelling went on, and many bodies
from both sides still lie in sealed-up tunnels. The
ground here has been left fairly undisturbed, and
behind the hill is a well-preserved concrete bunker.
There are memorials here to Queen Victoria's Rifles,
1st/9th Battalion The London Regiment and the 1st
Australian Tunnelling Company.

Return to Zillebekestraat and turn left towards
Ypres, continuing through Zillebeke village. There
are several cemeteries in this area. It is about 1 km.
to the crossroads . . . This is Hellfire Corner.

Hellfire Corner
The most notorious place in the Salient. Here the
Potijze–Zillebeke Road crosses the Menen Road, and
since it was an important route junction it was under
constant observation by the Germans on the high
ground beyond, who had heavy guns ranged upon
it. Anything that moved was fired upon, and canvas
screens were erected by the road to conceal
movement. To the right is a demarcation stone that
once stood by the road; it was damaged, and was
moved back to a safer position near by.

Turn left towards Ypres. On your left is Menen
Road South Military Cemetery, which now contains
all the bodies from the 'North' Cemetery that once
stood facing it.

Return to Ypres.

ITINERARY 2

Again the best place to start is from the Grote Markt
in Ypres. Take the Bruges (Brugge) exit and follow
the signs to Poelkapelle. Go past the Brooding
Soldier on the N 313; to the left you can see the

spire of Langemark Church. As you come into the village of Poelkapelle you will see the Guynemer Memorial straight ahead in the centre of the road. Park on the right by the Café-Guynemer.

Guynemer Memorial, Poelkapelle

With fifty-four 'kills' to his credit, Captain Georges Guynemer, Légion d'Honneur, was the most popular of French air aces. He was killed in September 1917, having been in action for two years. His squadron was known as 'The Storks', and the stork which surmounts the memorial, so it is said, is facing the direction in which Guynemer was flying on the day he died. The memorial dates from 1923, and there is also a memorial to the pilot in Compiègne, where he went to school.

Poelkapelle was captured by the Germans in October 1914, and remained in their hands for most of the war, although for a brief period during Third Ypres in 1917 it formed part of the British front line. The village was finally retaken by the Belgian army at the end of September 1918.

Continue in the same direction on the N 313. On the right, about ½ km. on, is a cemetery.

Poelkapelle British Cemetery

This was made after the Armistice by concentrating graves from surrounding areas, including Langemark and St Jan. In this cemetery is the grave of the youngest British soldier to die in the war: killed during Second Ypres in 1915, Private J. Condon was fourteen years old.*

* The oldest soldier to die in action was Lt H. Webber, aged 68, South Lancashire Regiment, killed during the Battle of the Somme, 1916. He is buried in Dartmoor Cemetery, Bécordel, near the town of Albert.

He was one of many who joined the army under age. In those first heady days of high summer in 1914, just after the outbreak of war, many young men – and even boys – lied about their ages in order to join up and share in what was widely seen as a great adventure, before it was all over. Given the fevered atmosphere of the time, this is not hard to understand; and with the connivance of a recruiting sergeant who kept any doubts he might have entertained about an applicant's real age to himself, and a doctor harassed by the press of would-be recruits coming for medical examination, anyone determined to serve who looked old enough did not find it difficult to enlist . . . And in the last resort, refusal at one recruiting centre did not mean that one could not try elsewhere and be successful.

One man recalls his own experience:

On the night of 1 September 1914, when I enlisted in Kitchener's Army, the war of 1914–1918 was barely a month old and my eighteenth birthday was just approaching. I was far from being the youngest recruit, for in the queue was a boy of fifteen who lost his life on the Somme a couple of years later.[21]

Another young soldier, C. J. Arthur, was fifteen when the war started. He at once joined his School Cadet Battalion, and was soon made a corporal. Then, as he wrote later:

At Whitsun, 1915, I told the O.C. [Officer Commanding] Cadets I was going to join up. 'Good,' he said. 'How old do you want to be?'

Formalities were swiftly completed. Arthur enlisted, became a sergeant in ten weeks, and was serving in France, wounded and awarded the Military Medal before he was eighteen.[22]

As the war proceeded fewer young men were prepared to come into the army before they had to. For one thing, the tide of jingoistic patriotism had begun to ebb quite noticeably by the second half of 1915; and then there was the introduction of compulsory military service in January 1916. But, of course, throughout the war there were always some who, for whatever reason, wanted to be fighting soldiers under the legal age, and Private Condon was unique in being the youngest of them to die.

Turn round, return to the Guynemer Memorial and take the right-hand road to Langemark.

Langemark
Turn right at the traffic lights and follow signs to the right of the church indicating 'Deutsche Soldaten Friedhof' (German Military Cemetery). Park on the left.

A German cemetery

Langemark was captured by the Germans during the first gas attack in April 1915, and retaken by the British during Third Ypres. When the Allies withdrew in spring 1918, the Germans occupied it again. Finally, the Belgians took it at the end of September 1918.

The German cemetery has two small rooms at its entrance. In the one on the left there is a Visitors' Book and a relief map showing past and present German cemeteries in Belgium. In the other room are oak panels upon which are carved the names of the missing. The cemetery is in two sections: the older part contains 10,143 graves, of which 3,836 are of unidentified German soldiers; in the newer part 24,834 men are buried in a mass grave in a fairly small area covered by shrubs. Watching over them is a bronze group which represents their mourning comrades. On the boundary walls are inscribed the insignia of the student battalions that served in the area. At the northern end of the cemetery are three concrete bunkers with linking memorial stones indicating the position of the Langemark defensive line. There are 9,475 men buried here; and in all, some 44,000 burials are recorded.

Return to the traffic lights and then turn right towards Boezinge. As you leave the village there is a memorial to the British on the right, then shortly afterwards Cement House Cemetery, named after a fortification that stood near by. Burials began here in August 1917 during the Third Battle of Ypres, and include soldiers from the United Kingdom, Canada, Newfoundland and Guernsey – nearly 3,000 graves.

As you travel along the road to Boezinge you are

'Telephonists at Work'. Artillery telephonists at Langemark, 21 August 1917. In their dug-out, about a quarter of a mile from the German line, they are passing messages from forward observation officers to gun batteries in the rear

moving in the same direction as the chlorine gas cloud which caused panic among the French colonial troops on 22 April 1915. Just after the cemetery you can see the spires of Ypres, and to their right, on the horizon, Kemmel Hill. Continue on the same road, crossing the Yser/IJzer Canal and the new major road, and enter the village of Boezinge. Stop before the T-junction.

Boezinge Village

Notice the Demarcation Stone with the French helmet, slightly to the right of the junction, and a blockhouse with a German mortar on top just behind it. Turn left towards Ypres. The ground as you leave the village is low and wet, and the line of trees indicates the course of the canal that, during most of the war, faced the German front line. The banks were fortified, and surviving concrete bunkers can still be seen occasionally. On the right you will pass

THE RAID

"Bert it's our officer"

Talana Farm Cemetery, with British and French burials. Next comes Bard Cottage Cemetery, begun in June 1915 during Second Ypres. To your left, just before the road goes under the bridge that carries the Ypres ring road, is Essex Farm Cemetery.

Essex Farm Cemetery

A small house stands to the left of the cemetery, and behind it, on privately owned land, there are some concrete dug-outs. Between 1915 and 1917 these were used as dressing stations, and during the Third Battle of Ypres, Scots and Welsh casualties from the 51st and 38th Divisions were amongst the many soldiers treated here. The cemetery has burials from the 38th, and more than 1,000 men altogether are buried here, including five German prisoners of war and some of the dead from the 49th (West Riding) Division, whose memorial column is behind the German graves, upon the canal bank.

It was in this area that the Canadian Medical Officer, Colonel John McCrae, wrote his poem 'In Flanders Fields'. He died during the influenza epidemic of 1918, and is buried at Wimereux, near Boulogne.

Continue under the road bridge and return to Ypres.

Grote Markt, Ypres

Leave by the exit signposted Poperinge Road, the N 308, and follow signs to Poperinge over the railway line. This point, where road and rail cross the canal, used to be known as Devil's Bridge. Several hundred metres further on, to the right, is Ypres Asylum, now rebuilt after its destruction by shellfire. The Poperinge Road was the route by which supplies of all kinds were brought into the Salient, and consequently it was much bombarded by enemy guns sited in the Flanders hills, which can be seen in the distance on the left. The result of the bombardment was that, like the town itself, the outskirts of and approaches to Ypres became something of a wilderness. Nevertheless, there were many dressing stations for the wounded, and other army units and depots, in this area.

Continue to Vlamertinge, take the second turning on the right immediately after the church, and stop 100 m. down the road.

Vlamertinge Military Cemetery

More than 200 casualties from the 55th (West Lancashire) Division are buried here. Return to the church junction, turn right, and continue towards Poperinge.

Vlamertinge. Hop Store Cemetery

At the end of the war Vlamertinge consisted for the most part of piles of rubble and a battered church. However, the hop store, a tall red-brick building, was beyond the normal range of enemy artillery fire, and the building survived – as you can see it today. The cemetery contains over 240 burials.

The road goes on past the Brandhoek cemeteries, sited round an area where there was a Field Ambulance throughout the war. Also close by are Red Farm Cemetery and Hagle Dump Cemetery. In Brandhoek New Military Cemetery No. 3 there is the grave of Captain N. G. Chavasse, V C, M C, Royal Army Medical Corps. He was Medical Officer to the 1st Battalion The Liverpool Scottish Regi-

'In the Front Line'. Men from the Honourable Artillery Company (HAC) in an infantry role cleaning their rifles in a front-line trench near St Eloois (Saint-Eloi). The photograph is dated April 1915, so they have not yet been issued with steel helmets

ment, and he died from wounds on 4 August 1917, the only man during the war to win the Victoria Cross and a Bar to it on the Western Front. His headstone in the cemetery (Plot III Grave B15) is unique, for it has on it two small representations of the VC instead of the usual larger one.

Captain Chavasse won his Military Cross at Hooge in 1915. Then, during the Battle of the

Somme in 1916, at Guillemont, he was awarded the
VC for conspicuous bravery and devotion to duty.
During an attack he looked after wounded men who
were lying out in the open all day and under heavy
fire, often in full view of the enemy. For four hours
during the night he searched for wounded in front
of the German line. On the following day,
accompanied by a stretcher-bearer, he went beyond
the British line and, again under heavy fire, carried
back a badly wounded man who was urgently in
need of treatment – a distance of 500 yards. While
doing so, Captain Chavasse was wounded in his side
by a shell splinter; but the same night he took twenty
volunteers and rescued three wounded men from a
shell hole 25 yards from the German trench. He
and his party buried two dead officers and, although
fired on by machine-guns and bombs, collected
many identity discs from dead soldiers. 'Altogether',
says his citation, 'he saved the lives of some twenty
badly wounded men, besides the ordinary cases
which passed through his hands. His courage and
self-sacrifice were beyond praise.'

On 14 September 1917, during the Third Battle of
Ypres, he was posthumously awarded a Bar to his
VC. The citation speaks of 'most conspicuous
bravery and devotion to duty'. Severely wounded
while carrying a wounded man to a dressing station,
he stayed at his post for two days, performing his
duty and going out repeatedly under heavy fire to
search for and tend wounded men. Despite lack of
food, fatigue and weakness caused by his wound, he
helped to carry in badly wounded men over heavy
and difficult ground. 'By his extraordinary energy
and inspiring example, he was instrumental in rescu-
ing many wounded who would have otherwise

undoubtedly succumbed under the bad weather conditions,' says his citation. Captain Chavasse died of his wounds in Brandhoek Military Hospital.*

This area had many military installations. Besides casualty clearing stations and hospitals there were, on all sides, temporary huts and tents, supply dumps of various kinds, horse lines, military police posts – and, inevitably, a forest of signs directing the newcomer to his destination.

Continue until the N 308 meets the new Poperinge ring road. Turn left, signposted to Cassel, then turn left again, shortly after passing the junction with the D 948, into Abeelsweg. At No. 70 a private collector, Monsieur Blankhard, has a considerable collection of army relics and memorabilia, which can be seen by appointment.

After 200 m. take a left turn, signposted to Lijssenthoek Military Cemetery. The road goes over a new waterway and over the route of the old single-track railway – now without its rails – which was used to move soldiers and supplies.

Lijssenthoek Military Cemetery

With about 10,000 burials, this is the second largest Allied war cemetery after Tyne Cot. Some Germans are included, as well as the British, French, American and Chinese burials, the headstones of the latter with inscriptions in Chinese characters as well as English. Many of these deaths date from April 1919, and were perhaps caused by an explosion when the

---

* There was another doctor, Lt. Arthur Martin-Leake, Royal Army Medical Corps, who won the VC twice, but the first was awarded to him in 1902 during the Boer War. The second was at Zonnebeke, near Ypres, in 1915 when he rescued, under fire, a number of wounded men lying near the enemy trenches.

Chinese Labour Corps were carrying out their work of clearing the battlefields after hostilities had ceased.

Return to Abeelsweg and turn left towards France.

L'Abeele and the Border

Follow the N 333 to the Belgian customs post at L'Abeele; between here and the French customs post at Steenvoorde the road, now the D 948, runs for some way along the border of the two countries. Look out for Aerodrome Cemetery, named after a Royal Flying Corps field. In France continue along the D 948 to Cassel.

Cassel

As the road climbs up the hill towards the town, it becomes cobbled and both looks and feels much as it must have done to British soldiers on the march.* Just before reaching the central square (Place Général de Gaulle) the road becomes the Rue du Maréchal Foch. Half-way up the square on the left is a clearly signposted museum.

Standing in the square, you are roughly at the centre of the highest town in Flanders – 176 m. Possession of the hill has been much contested for something like 2,000 years, ever since the Romans took it over from the Celts and turned its summit into a fortress – a 'castellum', from which the town's name is derived. During the war there was much

---

* And not only during the Great War! This is the hill up (and down) which the Grand Old Duke of York marched his men during the Flanders campaign of 1793–4, when a British contingent led by the Duke was beaten by the French revolutionary army.

coming and going of notables. Early on, Marshal Foch had an HQ here, and was visited by King George V, the Belgian King, the Prince of Wales and General Sir Douglas Haig. Sir John French, first commander of the British Expeditionary Force, had an HQ here, and so later did General Plumer, who commanded the Second Army. It was here in Cassel that Marshal Foch held the conference that laid plans for what turned out to be the final offensive of the war.

The museum is a Renaissance-style building dating from the close of the sixteenth century. Although the contents are mostly connected with the art, history and folklore of the region, Marshal Foch had his office here, and it is now preserved with a good deal of Foch memorabilia. The museum is open every Sunday afternoon in the summer, or can be opened at other times on request at the Town Hall (Mairie), which is opposite. The old Mairie, dating from 1634, was destroyed by the German Air Force in 1940, so the building is a new one. Tourist information is available.

Continue walking up the Chemin du Château (or the steep steps near by) to the highest point in the town – the summit of Mont Cassel, upon which the town is built – and come to the Jardin Public (Public Garden), which contains a statue of Marshal Foch, created by Georges Malissard and unveiled in 1928. It faces towards Ypres and Menen, and orientation marks are set into the low walls. (There is a replica of it in Grosvenor Gardens, near Victoria Station in London, in the area that during the war contained a tented transit camp used by soldiers on their way to and from the continent.) Near the statue are the remains of a concrete bunker below which were underground offices.* Beyond is a memorial to the battles of Cassel in 1677, which were a victory for the French. From here, on a clear day and with binoculars, it is possible to distinguish the spires of Ypres and even the pillars of the Vimy Ridge Memorial.

With a map obtainable from the Mairie it is well worth while to walk around the town – which is not very large – and particularly around the ramparts encircling it. At one time there were twenty-four windmills on Mont Cassel. Only one survives now, and it is open to the public.

Returning to your car, drive back down the hill and across the frontier at L'Abeele. As you go along this route towards Poperinge (N 333), recall that you are travelling in precisely the same direction as the hundreds of thousands of soldiers who fought in the Salient, with their supporting hospitals, hutted and tented camps, depots and dumps crowding the countryside. They passed through in great numbers, from various regiments and corps; and consequently 'back' areas like this were constantly patrolled by military police, and any soldier found more than a few miles from his unit without authorization was liable to arrest.

The town of Poperinge was the last recognizable one before reaching the devastation that fighting had made of Ypres and the surrounding villages. Stop in Poperinge and park in the Grote Markt.

Poperinge
A thriving and very old town, 'Pop', as it was known to the many English-speaking soldiers who thronged

---

* Originally they were cellars beneath the castle on this site, which has long since disappeared.

its narrow streets, was the forward base for the Ypres Salient. Behind the town there were innumerable military installations, but these have left hardly any trace on the landscape.*

Poperinge was also a centre for the relaxation of men coming out of the trenches. The hectic activity and crowds of those days were very different from the sleepy air of the town today. Here, as ever in the back areas of France and Flanders, there were premises offering the inevitable 'Eggs, Fish, Chips, Tea', besides canteens run by voluntary organizations like the Y M C A. Semi-official 'Expeditionary Force Canteens' did not come into being until 1915. One of the pleasures of 'Pop' for soldiers coming tired and dirty out of the line was the possibility of having a bath or shower in the vats of the brewery in the square. Thousands of troops would have used this facility, and the one at Vlamertinge not far away. Despite the fact that the water was often tepid, the showers were a mere dribble, and batches of men were hustled through the baths very quickly indeed, the process must have been a great relief to men who had not had their clothes off their backs for some time, nor taken off their boots. This was

* Except, of course, for the military cemeteries. Three of these, a few kilometres north-west of Poperinge, have names coined by British troops which sound like local Flemish usage: Mendinghem, Dozinghem and Bandaghem. The first was the site of No. 61 Casualty Clearing Station. To it were brought, as prisoners, men at the end of their tether who were desperate enough to shoot off their trigger finger, blast a hole in their foot or otherwise mutilate themselves to avoid 'going over the top' into battle. (S I W — self-inflicted wound — was the official abbreviation, and it constituted a serious offence against military law.) They would be nursed under guard until they were sufficiently recovered to be tried by Court Martial, with its inevitable punishment of imprisonment.

the occasion when clean underwear and socks were
issued and soiled garments handed in for washing
and reissue to someone else. An anonymous soldier
recalling 'bath parade' asked whether 'anyone recalls
receiving baby socks and giant pants, and if he had
cause to suspect that a clean vest could harbour
lice'.[23]

Poperinge had been taken by the Germans on 4
October 1914, but they were driven out eleven days
later and the town saw no more fighting – although
it was occasionally shelled by German heavy guns
such as 'Whistling Rufus', sited on a railway line
beyond Ypres.

Stand in the middle of the square and imagine

*AT THE
BREWERY
BATHS.
"You chuck
another sardine
at me, my
lad, and
you'll hear from
my solicitors"*

yourself at the centre of a clock face. Face the Café de la Paix, which is at 12 o'clock. Behind you, at 6 o'clock, is the Stadhuis, or Hôtel de Ville (Town Hall), easily distinguishable by its church-like tower. At 7 o'clock are Saint-Bertin's Church and the war memorial. At 10 o'clock, No. 16 is the Café De Ranke. Since the town is small, walking is the best way to see it.

The Stadhuis is Neo-Gothic, built in 1911. During the war it was used as a Divisional Headquarters. It was damaged by intermittent German shelling of the town, but today it is beautifully restored and in it, up a short flight of steps, there is an information office where town maps and guides are available.

The Café De Ranke was very famous during the war, being known as 'Ginger's' (the café was run by Madame Cossey and her three red-haired daughters), and later as 'À la Poupée'. The café was open to officers only: while death and mutilation came quite impartially to officers and men alike in the trenches, once out of the line distinctions of rank were rigidly enforced. Non-commissioned officers and men were forbidden to enter places designated 'Officers Only'.

Walk up Gasthuisstraat on the left. No. 12 ('Skindles') was a café originally called the 'Café de la Commerce des Houblons' (Hop Market Café), but the French name proved too difficult for the British and Commonwealth officers who patronized it, and one of them, seeing a resemblance to Skindles Hotel in Maidenhead, Berkshire, suggested the name. Madame Beutin, the proprietor, adopted this name, and it eventually became widely known. After the war 'Skindles' moved to No. 57.

No. 26, Hôtel Cyrille, no longer a hotel, was during the war another officer-only establishment. It was destroyed by a direct hit from a German shell during the offensive of March 1918, and has been rebuilt.

No. 43, Talbot House, named after Gilbert Talbot, who was killed in the Salient in July 1915 and is buried in Sanctuary Wood Cemetery,* is where the Rev. Philip Byard ('Tubby') Clayton started a movement that was to become world-wide: 'Toc H', so named from army signallers' version of the initial letters of the house's name.

Talbot House was opened on 11 December 1915 as an all-ranks club† under the supervision of 'Tubby' Clayton. Here, away from the noise and ugliness of war, men could come and relax in comparative comfort, enjoy the garden, write letters home, be quiet, or simply drink tea and chat . . . In the upper room, in what had once been a hop and fruit attic, there was a small chapel used between 1915 and 1918 by more than 25,000 men and women. One of the rooms contained a miscellaneous collection of books that could be borrowed. Once the choice had been made, borrowers had to leave their cap with the librarian as hostage against the book's return. In theory this precaution meant no losses; but 'Tubby' Clayton recalled that after the war books were sent back to him from prison camps in Prussia!

The house remained open until May 1918, when enemy shellfire caused its closure for a few months.

---

* He was the brother of Neville Talbot, an army chaplain who had been instrumental in securing the premises.

† An original sign in the house reads 'Abandon rank all ye that enter here'.

It reopened at the end of September 1918, but in January 1919 the original owner reclaimed the premises, the club closed down, and it was not until 1926 that the owner could eventually be persuaded to allow visitors. Then in 1929 Lord Wakefield purchased the house on behalf of Toc H, and its doors were soon open again. Today reasonably priced accommodation is available, there are original artefacts to be seen, and the chapel has hardly changed over the years. Housekeepers are in residence, and visits can be made on most days at reasonable hours.

In the meantime the Toc H Christian movement, founded in 1919, perpetuated the name of the house where it all started in Poperinge. It was designed to help men and women who, after the war, looked in vain for jobs, and also to keep alive what was called 'the brotherhood of the trenches'. The present writer remembers with pleasure the canteens provided by Toc H during the Second World War. 'Tubby' Clayton, who constantly visited Talbot House during his lifetime, died in 1972.

No. 57, although now a private house, is the site to which Skindles moved after the war, and still bears the café's name. Many visitors to the Salient stayed here after the war, and until the very last years of the hotel an early map showing the location of British war cemeteries hung in the dining-room.

Return to the Grote Markt and leave Poperinge via Gasthuisstraat, returning to Ypres via the N 308. On the way you will pass Poperinge railway station on the right. This was probably the most loved, and simultaneously the most feared, spot in the town. Leave trains left from here, and the station was always thronged with soldiers awaiting them: men returning to the front did not linger here. Rumour had it that the station master had been shot as a German spy, so regular was the shelling!

Continue to Ypres via Vlamertinge. In this village a large roadside notice erected in 1916 warned: 'Tin hats must be worn from here onward'.

ITINERARY 3

It is a good idea to begin by walking around Ypres. Leave the Grote Markt by Rijselstraat. On the left at No. 83, near the bus stop, there is a convent. This is the site of 'Little Toc H': from November 1917 to April 1918 Ypres was evacuated by all but fighting units, and during this period all the facilities of the Poperinge house were matched here.

Lille Gate (Rijselpoort)
Because the Menin Gate was so exposed, most troops went into the Salient through the Lille Gate, which still bears some scars from the war. On the left, under the arch, is a doorway that once led to a small museum, and before that to the dug-outs with which all the ramparts were riddled. It is said that Canadian tunnelling companies used these. The towers of the gate date from around 1395, and the ramparts themselves were rebuilt under the direction of Vauban, the famous French military engineer, in the seventeenth century. Climb up to the ramparts on the right.

Ramparts Cemetery
Started by the French in 1914, this is one of the smallest cemeteries in the Salient, recording 193 burials. Cross over to the other side of the Gate and

walk along the ramparts to the Menin Gate, noting remains of old shelters and machine-gun emplacements marking a defensive line of trenches once running all along the top of the ramparts. Descend and walk along the Menin Road back to your car, leaving Ypres through the Lille Gate and following signs to Rijsel (Lille) on the N 365. In 1½ km. you will reach Shrapnel Corner.

Shrapnel Corner

This crossing area was heavily shelled by the Germans. As at Hellfire Corner, a good deal of supply traffic passed this way, particularly at night, when ammunition and rations were taken up to the line.

Continue towards Lille. About 1 km. further, on the left, is Bedford House.

Bedford House Cemetery

Originally called Rosendael Château, the ruins of which form an integral part of the cemetery, this is one of the largest burial grounds in the Salient, with plots from 1939–45 as well as from 1914–18. About ½ km. further on, to the left, are some concrete bunkers.

Lankhof Farm Bunkers

There is a cluster of British concrete bunkers in the grounds of the farm. This is private property on a small island to the left; and since they are used by the farmer for his cattle they cannot be visited.

Continue on the N 365, taking the right fork at St Eloois and following the signs for Armentières and Mesen (Messines). Away to your right, Kemmel Hill can be seen from here. Follow the road to Wijtschate

THE SENTRY

*What he doesn't know about fire buckets and the time the rum
comes up isn't worth knowing*

('Whitesheet' to the BEF). As you enter the town there is a crossroads; turn right towards Kemmel, continue into the square, keep right past the bandstand, then at the Café du Centre turn right down Poperingestraat. Three hundred metres after passing a football field on the left, you enter some woods, and almost immediately there is a road junction to the right with a sign for Croonaert Chapel Cemetery. Turn right on to Voormezelestraat, and in about 1 km. you come to a museum.

Museum of Peace

Privately owned by Monsieur A. Becquart, this museum is open all the year round during daylight hours. A small fee is charged for admission. It has a fascinating collection of wartime relics, some of which can be purchased. In addition there are trench lines, shell holes and an old mine shaft that is usually full of water.

Opposite the museum, beyond the car park, are some earthworks dating from earlier times, and some trenches in which Adolf Hitler is reputed to have served as a soldier. He drew some sketches in this area.

Return to the N 365 and turn right towards Messines, about 2 km. away.

Messines (Mesen) Church

The church can be seen to the left on a sharp right-hand bend as you go through the village. It is rather a squat building that has been entirely rebuilt. The village is on high ground which is a continuation of the ridge that sweeps round to Passchendaele in the north-east.

This area, the Messines Ridge, was the scene of

much heavy fighting, and there are several memorials and cemeteries that can all be easily located
from signs. The Germans took the ridge in
November 1914 and held it until they were driven
out by the New Zealand Division in June 1917 – it
was the New Zealanders' preliminary bombardment
that laid waste the entire village. On 10 April 1918
the Germans recaptured it for a few hours, were
forced out by the South African Brigade, retook it
the following day, and held it until they were finally
ejected on 28 September 1918.

As you leave the village the road descends and
then rises to a crest where signposts indicate
Ploegsteert Wood ('Plugstreet' to the BEF) and
other memorials and cemeteries to the left. Continue
straight ahead for about 400 m. and stop on the
right near the British Cemetery at Hyde Park
Corner.

Hyde Park Corner/Royal Berks. Cemetery

The Ploegsteert Memorial to the Missing and Berks.
Corner Cemetery Extension are guarded by two
lions, one of them snarling his defiance. The original
cemetery is opposite. The memorial, a rotunda-like
structure, is unique in the Salient. It was designed
by H. Charlton Bradshaw and the sculptor was Sir
Gilbert Ledward. It was unveiled in June 1931. On
the panels within the colonnade 11,447 names are
recorded: these are the missing from the battles of
Armentières, Aubers Ridge (1914), Loos-Fromelles
(1915), Estaires (1916), Hazebrouck, Scherpenberg
and Outtersteene Ridge (1918). Over 380 men are
buried in the cemetery.

The original cemetery on the left was started by
the 1st/4th Battalion The Royal Berkshire Regiment

during Second Ypres in 1915. Beyond it, to the left, you can see Ploegsteert Wood, the scene of heavy fighting, particularly during the First Battle of Ypres in 1914; but the Germans were never able to take the wood.

It was in this area that Bruce Bairnsfather drew his first war cartoons and 'Old Bill' was born (see footnote, p. 88).

Continue, passing Strand Cemetery on your left, to the crossroads in Ploegsteert village. This remained behind British lines until April 1918, and then was recaptured in September.

Turn left at the crossroads signposted towards Lancashire Cottage Cemetery. In 2 km., within Ploegsteert Wood, there is a house with bunkers beside it, in trees at the edge of the road. Inquire at the house if you wish to visit them.

Turn around and return to the crossroads, continuing straight over, following the signs to Nieuwkerke (Neuve-Église) and Kemmel. After Nieuwkerke, follow the signs to Ieper (Ypres), then Kemmelberg, and uphill past a sign to Lindenhoek Chalet Military Cemetery on the left, then downhill to Kemmel village crossroads. Turn left here and follow the signs to Kemmelberg and the Ossuaire Français. Take the second left, and keep right of the bandstand and left of In de Wandeling Café. At the crest of the hill, opposite a car park, turn sharp right up a cobbled road to the Hostellerie Belvedere Restaurant.

Kemmel Hill and Belvedere Café

The hill remained in British hands until April 1918, and was retaken at the end of August. The fighting round Kemmel Hill exemplifies the importance that was attached to the possession of high ground. It is both easier to defend – an infantry attack uphill was always a costly and hazardous affair – and a good observation point. All the hills and ridges around Ypres were the scene of heavy fighting, and the German possession of so much of this high ground put the Allied armies at a continuing disadvantage.

The tower on the Belvedere – a rebuilt and rather different version of the original destroyed during the war – is open to visitors from the end of April to the end of September. For a small admission fee you can climb it and look right over the Salient towards Ypres. The view is superb.

Continue up the hill to the French Memorial.

Memorial to the French Soldiers, 1918

This column and the winged figure at its base commemorate the fallen of the battles for the Flanders hills in 1918. There is a more general memorial plaque to all the French who fell in the Salient on the Cloth Hall at Ypres.

Continue 200 m. downhill to the French Cemetery.

French National Cemetery, Kemmel

The cockerel standing on its column marks the ossuary where 5,294 officers and men are buried. Of this total a mere fifty-seven have been identified.

Continue to the next small crossroads and turn right, following signs to Kemmel. Go left past the bandstand,* down Polenlaan to a T-junction, and

---

* Where various regimental bands, including that of the Brigade of Guards, gave concerts during lulls in the fighting.

then right. In 200 m. you come to Kemmel cross-roads. Go straight over for 2 km., and at a small turning to the right is a sign for Lone Tree Cemetery (Spanbroekmolen). A short distance up the turning you will see a large water-filled hole measuring 80 m. in diameter and 12 m. deep. This is the site of what was almost certainly the largest explosion of the nineteen caused by British mines in the Messines fighting at the beginning of Third Ypres in 1917. The site was purchased by Lord Wakefield for Toc H and now, untouched, it is a memorial named the Pool of Peace.

Return to the crossroads and turn right towards Ypres. About 1 km. on is La Laiterie Cemetery on the left; and 600 m. further on is the American Monument.

American Monument

This is a rectangular white block, in front of which a soldier's helmet rests upon a laurel wreath. It commemorates the Americans of the 27th and 30th Divisions who fought with British forces in the surrounding area in the late summer of 1918.

'Doughboy' –
American soldier

Continue to the next crossroads and turn left by the Café de Vierstraat along Kleine Vierstraat in the direction of Dikkebus. There was heavy fighting in this area during the German April 1918 assault, and several cemeteries are signposted. Continue over the first crossroads on Hallebaststraat, and turn right at the next crossroads in Hallebast by the Hallebast Restaurant. Go through Dikkebus and turn right at the roadside café called Festival, where flags will probably be flying, beside a small waterway, and follow signs to Vijver Dikkebus Étang.

Dikkebus. Dickebusch Lake

Neither the village of Dikkebus nor the lake was ever taken by the Germans, although in May 1918 the fighting did reach the edge of the lake. There were rest camps here for troops out of the line. Worth seeing here, to the right of the path leading from the car park to the lakeside restaurant, is an old Vauban watch tower from the seventeenth century, and at the edge of the water some ramparts dating from 1678. There are railings here made of chain links suspended from shells. Beyond them, over the water, Kemmel Hill can be clearly seen.

Return to the main road, turn right, and follow signs for Ypres. About 2 km. further on is Belgian Battery Corner Cemetery, recording over 550 burials. Return to Ypres, passing the railway station, to the Grote Markt.

Loos, Vimy Ridge and Arras

If you are coming south from Ypres, leave on the N 365 via the Lille Gate (Rijselpoort) and follow the road to Le Bizet frontier post. Armentières is about 20 km. away – approach the town on the new D 22A. At the junction with the D 933 turn into the central square, the Place Général de Gaulle.

Armentières

The town, with its main industries connected with brewing and linen manufacture, was held briefly by the Germans in 1914, but by October of that year the British had recaptured it and held it for the next three and a half years. Situated as it was just behind the line, it was used by the army as a base and as a recreation centre, despite intermittent bombing and shelling. The damage from this was slight, and Armentières was not destroyed until October 1918, when the retreating Germans, who had re-entered the town during their final offensive in April, were driven out by the British. Before leaving, the Germans mined or destroyed all the main buildings and the factories. During the long British occupation of the town the central square was known as 11 o'Clock Square, because a stray German shell had damaged the clock on the Hôtel de Ville and stopped it at this time.

For some unaccountable reason Armentières gave its name to one of the famous songs of the Great War. In its best-known form, to the tune of a French music hall ditty, it went like this:

> Mademoiselle from Armenteers,
> Parley-vous!
> Mademoiselle from Armenteers,
> Parley-vous!
> Mademoiselle from Armenteers,
> She hasn't been — for forty years,
> Inky-pinky parley-vous.

The song was popular with the BEF and was adopted by American troops arriving in France in 1918. It went back with them to the USA, where differing versions of it were sung at veterans' gatherings after the war.

Leave Armentières via the Rue de Lille, then the Rue de Béthune (D 22). Shortly after leaving the town cross the motorway and continue on the D 22B for 5 km. to Fleurbaix. Continue on the D 171 for 3 km. to Pétillon crossroads, turn left on to the D 175/22C, and in 1 km. you come to V C Corner Australian Memorial and Cemetery, Fromelles.

'Christmas Day: How it dawned for many'

The cemetery is unusual, as there are no headstones. The dead were brought here after the end of the war from the surrounding areas of fighting, and over 400 are buried here – one of the very few Allied mass burial plots. The Australian Memorial to the Missing records 1,299 names.

Continue along the road, bearing left at the fork, and come into Fromelles. Turn right at the D 141, bearing right through Aubers and come to Fauquissart. Turn left on to the D 171. The area you have just passed through gives little indication that

it was once a battleground. South from Pétillon the road follows roughly what was the 1914–15 line, and it was in this neighbourhood that the 1914 Christmas truce between the opposing front-line soldiers took place.*

After so long it is difficult to disentangle truth from fiction in the matter of fraternization between the opposing armies at Christmas 1914. Without any doubt at all some mingling, with exchange of souvenirs, cigarettes and even rations, took place in no-man's land between the trenches: what is equally

* An incident that was vividly dramatized in Joan Littlewood's musical, *Oh, What a Lovely War!*.

true is that such isolated episodes gave rise to an enduring myth. The actual events were probably quite prosaic. A sergeant in the 2nd Battalion Wiltshire Regiment remembered seeing a Christmas tree on the parapet of an enemy trench, and told how two Germans with a white flag came to within fifty yards of his position and asked for a British officer who could speak German. There was one – and a two-day truce was arranged.[24] In other areas, perhaps, things were done differently.

Continue 3 km. to Neuve-Chapelle, where the Indian Corps first went into action in October 1914 and where Indian troops were also in action in March of the following year. The Indian Memorial is 1 km. further on at La Bombe crossroads; and a few yards down the D 947 is the Portuguese Military Cemetery.

This rather dull road (still the D 171) is just behind what was the front of the Indian Corps during the battles of Festubert and Aubers Ridge in 1915. The role of Indian troops on the Western Front has not always received the attention that it deserves. Two Indian divisions reached Marseilles towards the end of September 1914. They were issued with a new pattern of rifle, and some were in the fighting line a fortnight later. In that autumn of 1914 the British held one tenth of the Allied line, and the Indians held one third of this. Despite the fact that they were trained for frontier warfare in their own country, with a climate to which they were accustomed and where they would expect to face snipers' bullets and the onrush of attacking tribesmen, they endured high-explosive shells, machine-guns, mortars and liquid fire with re- markably stoicism; and furthermore, even though some of them were wearing khaki drill uniforms until Christmas, there was the continuous damp cold of the trenches. In a number of crucial actions they fought the enemy with outstanding courage.[25]

To single out the Indians like this is in no way to denigrate the valiant achievements of other troops from the then British Empire. Australians, Canadians and New Zealanders were all present on the Western Front in large numbers long after the Indian Corps – for reasons quite unconnected with their fighting ability – had been withdrawn to Mesopotamia; and the Indians' exploits, at Neuve-Chapelle or Loos for example, passed into legend.

A few kilometres further on is Le Touret British Cemetery, where the Memorial to the Missing is for those who fell at Festubert and Aubers Ridge, and also at La Bassée and Neuve-Chapelle.

Just beyond the cemetery turn right on to a small road which goes to Richebourg; then turn left at the junction with the D 170 until you come to La Couture. In front of the village church there is a somewhat unusual Portuguese Memorial. Come back the way you have arrived. At the main road turn left, then shortly after right on to the D 166 for Festubert.

Festubert

The village was the scene of fighting in 1914 and April 1918 – on the latter occasion it was the defence of Festubert and Givenchy, the next village, that checked the German advance. By that time both villages, like most of the surrounding ones, were in ruins.

After passing Festubert church, notice on the left of the road a British blockhouse and bunker, which served at times both as a ration point and as an officers' dug-out. From 1919 until the early 1970s it was lived in by a Frenchwoman.

Two kilometres further on is Givenchy, scene of much fighting. The crossroads just before the village was called Windy Corner. There is a Guards Cemetery here.

Cross La Bassée Canal and enter Cuinchy, a front-line village that was completely destroyed. In January 1915 there was fierce fighting here, as the Guards Memorial recalls, and on the ground it is still possible to discern how severely it was cratered.

Cambrin, a straggling village, is 1 km. on. Come to the main road (N 41) and turn right for Béthune, 8 km. distant.

Béthune

Béthune is an old town, and was once the seat of the counts of Flanders. The belfry standing in the central square was built in 1346. The houses surrounding it were destroyed and have not been rebuilt, but others round the square have been rebuilt in a characteristic Flanders style. In 1914 Béthune was a prosperous town, a centre for the surrounding mines and market gardens. During the war it became a British headquarters town, and between 1915 and 1918 it was occasionally bombarded.

The Indian Corps held it from 1914 to 1915: there were corps and divisional headquarters here, it was an important railhead, and there was a good deal of military coming and going. In the German April 1918 offensive the town was pretty well destroyed. The church of St Waast was reduced to rubble, but the belfry survived; the top of it was dislodged, and that has been rebuilt in identical form, so that now only the great doors on the ground floor, made of glass, indicate that the belfry is not completely as it was.

Only part of the town fell to the Germans in 1918, three British divisions successfully holding the remainder against their advance. In the Second World War the town was again damaged.

The Battle of Loos

The battle was fought by the British, between 25 September and 13 October 1915, in support of the French offensive in Champagne. British casualties were enormous, and were suffered largely by soldiers who went into action only partially trained. The battle is also memorable for the fact that for the first time the British used poison gas. Although Loos was taken, gains in ground were inconsiderable.

Leave Béthune via the N 41, which joins the N 43 in about 3 km. The road crosses a plain, scattered with mines and slagheaps, and the southern sector of the Loos battlefields, which lie between the N 43, the D 947 (the old main road from La Bassée) and the new N 47. Ten kilometres down the road is Dud Corner Cemetery and the Loos Memorial to the Missing, where the names of 20,589 officers and men who died in this battle and on the Lys, Estaires and Béthune fronts in 1918 are recorded. Rudyard Kipling's son is one of the names on the Irish Guards panel.

Continue down the N 43 and then, if you have the time, in 2 km. take the D 165 to the left. It will bring you to the D 947, and if you stop here you can see Hill 70, one of the focal points of the battle to the south of Loos. Much of the battlefield round this area is covered by a huge hypermarket and a civilian airfield; but elsewhere it is still possible to discern the vestiges of trenches and craters. Return to the N 43, turn left and continue for $4\frac{1}{2}$ km. to Lens.

Lens

Before the war virtually destroyed it, Lens was the main coal-mining town in France. It is still a thriving industrial town and many of the mines are being worked, although the winding towers which were a feature of the landscape in 1914 are quickly disappearing. Lens was occupied by the Germans in October 1914, and they began at once to fortify it strongly. It became the centre of a war fought underground in tunnels driven through the earth by both sides. In August 1917 an Allied attack was launched from Hill 70 and the north-western suburbs, but the Germans succeeded in holding the centre of the town. There were further attacks in September 1917 and January 1918, but it was not until October that the town, in ruins, was captured.

Since it is today a very busy and crowded town with a complex road layout, you would do better to bypass it by joining the autoroute A 21 and travelling south-east, following the signs for Arras. Six kilometres further on, at Noyelles, the road to Arras becomes the N 17, but for the first 3 km. it resembles a motorway. About 1 km. further on, just after you have gone through the complex of the Union Chimique et Minière at Avion, the road swings round in a curve before the old road meets it again below Vimy Ridge, and you have a panoramic view of the twin-pillared Canadian Memorial high above the wooded slopes of Hill 145.

Vimy Ridge (Battle of Arras)

Continue for another 3 km., and at the Vimy/Givenchy-en-Gohelle crossroads turn right for Givenchy. The road beneath the escarpment is straight, and eventually climbs up through Givenchy.

This village marks the most northerly point of the 25 km. front upon which Allied troops launched their attack on 9 April 1917 in the opening stage of the Battle of Arras. As so often on the Western Front, the battle was indecisive and casualties on both sides were extremely high. The tactics used on the Somme in the preceding year – limited objectives, progress by slow stages, battles of attrition – still held sway . . . and the results were much the same. The Battle of Arras is chiefly recalled today for the storming of Vimy Ridge by four Canadian divisions, although it started with the capture by Allied forces of 13,000 prisoners and 200 pieces of artillery. By the end of April it had dwindled into a bloody stalemate.

Go through Givenchy, passing a concrete dugout, a German entrance to the maze of tunnels made by men of both sides – on the Allied slopes of the Ridge all these tunnels were used to conceal large concentrations of troops. Altogether there are twenty-two miles of subways at four quite distinct levels; and within this labyrinth there was room for accommodation, headquarters and stores. This vast operation had been started in 1915 by the French, and it was continued by the Germans, and later by

British, Canadian and Australian troops. Many of the tunnels were lit by electricity; water supplies were laid on; there were ventilation shafts; and there was a narrow-gauge railway.

As you swing left from Givenchy to the Memorial Park you will see on your right the French Memorial to the Moroccan troops who fought here in 1915. Bear to your left – the road behind the memorial is part of a one-way system running through the park, which is packed with shell holes. There is a large car park to your right and, next to the toilets, a large bronze map of the battlefield. The memorial can be reached via the footpaths that commence between two flagpoles on which Canadian and French flags fly. Don't miss the beavers at the base of each pole. The Superintendent's house and office are beyond the car park.

Walking or driving through the park, you will notice wired-off enclosures with warnings to visitors of danger from rusting shells and grenades in areas that have not yet been cleared. Those parts of the park which can be explored are clearly defined and signposted.

Next to Grange Tunnel is the Guides' Office, where postcards and literature* can be bought. The tunnel is open to the public during the summer months, and items of equipment are still lying about . . .

Some of the trench lines are clearly indicated, although because of the concrete 'sandbags' and duckboards they seem rather artificial and impossibly tidy. However, it is possible to gain here

---

* For tourists the best buy is almost certainly *Canada on Vimy Ridge* by Colonel A. F. Duguid. It contains, in addition to a clear account of the operations and afterwards, an excellent map.

some idea of the scale of the battlefield and the distance between the opposing lines – sometimes unbelievably short. Visitors are allowed to walk in the trenches, but this is not recommended for anyone wearing high-heeled shoes. Since the entire park is a memorial, neither picnics nor games of any kind are permitted.

One way to leave the park is via the road running above the trench sector. It skirts the southern edge of the park and joins the N 17 north of Thélus crossroads. Continue across the N 17 as far as the crossroads, turn left, and stop. You can see the Canadian Artillery Memorial that was unveiled on 9 April 1918, exactly a year after the capture of Vimy Ridge. A South African artillery battery that took part in the battle is remembered here too.

Thélus
Just beyond the village is the British Cemetery, and near by in fields where the vestiges of trenches can still be seen is the 1st Canadian Division Memorial, which was erected at Christmas 1917. Between March and July 1917 Canadian troops were heavily engaged in the neighbourhood, and there was more fighting in these wide fields when the Germans tried, unsuccessfully, to take Arras in March 1918.

Another 4 km. or so further on we come to Bailleul-Sire-Berthoult. This was a German front-line position taken after heavy fighting in April 1917. On the far side of the village follow an undesignated road on the left for Oppy, which is 3 km. away.

Oppy Wood
As you come near the village Oppy Wood is to your right. When the Germans occupied it they trans-

formed it into one of the major strongpoints of the
Western Front, and numerous attempts to capture it
failed. Eventually, after a bitter struggle with heavy
losses on both sides, the 8th Division took the wood
in September 1918. When the wood fell into British
hands the whole area was a sea of mud and destruction. It is now privately owned.

On the right of the road there is an unusual
monument to the men of Kingston upon Hull. Also
remembered is the son of the donor of the land
upon which it stands, who was killed on the Somme
in 1918.

Gavrelle
Continue on the D 33 to Gavrelle – this is still part
of the 1917 battlefield, and was the scene of an
attack by the 63rd Royal Naval Division. They took
the village and held it against continued counter-
attacks. It was held by successive British troops until
March 1918, when the 56th London Division defending it was overwhelmed. At the end of August
the 51st Highland Division retook it.

Turn right, then almost immediately left on to the
D 42E across the N 50. The road here goes through
the scenes of much fighting in 1917 and 1918.
Before reaching Fampoux you cross the motorway.

You are now in the Scarpe Valley. Fampoux, like
the neighbouring village of Rœux, saw severe
fighting both above and below ground. As the road
enters the village it joins another to the immediate
right. This is a very tight turn leading up York Road
(so named in 1917) towards the Celtic Cross of the
Seaforth Highlanders and the Sunken Cemetery of
the 4th Division on the crest of the ridge. On these

plains in 1917 the Scottish battalion was almost wiped out.

Keep on the same road until it meets the N 50 in the shadow of the motorway flyover, and turn left towards Arras. In 1 km. you will see the 9th Scottish Division HQ dug-out, now a memorial surrounded by a ring of trenches that have all but disappeared. Further along the road to the left is a British cemetery. Continue to Arras, 3 km. away. To the right is a German cemetery, and near by on the D 919 two British cemeteries.

In Arras you can park in the central square.

Arras

A very ancient city, once the capital of the Atrebates, from whom its name derives, Arras has long been the focal point of warring armies, and the modern city has been completely rebuilt after its virtual destruction in the Great War.

It was held briefly by the Germans in September 1914, but they were forced out by the French, and the small salient in the line formed by Arras was tenaciously defended by French and British garrisons. It also suffered a number of air raids; in November 1916 forty German aircraft bombed the city.

One of the reasons for the continuing resistance was that, although much of the town was in ruins, there were many underground cellars known as 'boves' in which both civilians and soldiers could take shelter. Arras never again fell into German hands, despite the ferocity of the 1918 assault.

In 1940 the British army was involved in a rearguard action here, and amongst the last soldiers to leave were the Welsh Guards. In August 1944 they were one of the first units to re-enter it.

The Hôtel de Ville, demolished by fire and by bombardment, has been beautifully rebuilt in the original fifteenth- and sixteenth-century style with more modern nineteenth-century wings. The belfry, completed in 1553, collapsed in October 1914, and this too has been splendidly restored. There are memorial plaques in the foyer; and outside, near the main entrance, is the 1939–44 Resistance Memorial.

There is a British Military Cemetery in the Faubourg d'Amiens, and the Arras Memorial to the Missing, a superb colonnade with the central monument dedicated to the Royal Flying Corps, Royal Naval Air Service and Royal Air Force. The memorial records 35,928 names of the missing from the battles of Arras, Vimy Ridge, the Scarfe, Arleux, Bullecourt and Hill 70. The Air Service Memorial contains the names of all their missing on the Western Front. In the cemetery there are more than 2,600 graves.

By the side of the memorial a narrow road leads to the moat of the Citadel. On the Mur des Fusilés there are 200 plaques recording the names of French patriots who were shot here by the Germans during their occupation of the city in the Second World War.

The
Somme

The Battle of the Somme – in fact, a series of battles – which took place between 1 July and 19 November 1916, was conceived as a joint British/French undertaking designed to resolve the trench deadlock on the Western Front. The idea was to strike a decisive blow at the Germans by breaking through their front line, then surging into the open country beyond Bapaume and inflicting a military defeat upon them, so bringing the war to an end. The Somme front was chosen – it was in this sector, near Maricourt, that the British and French lines met – and in this 'great offensive', as it was called, the two allies were to act simultaneously in what was anticipated to be the last offensive of the war. Seldom in history can such high hopes have come to nothing at so terrible a cost in human lives and suffering. In about four and a half months of fighting British losses were 420,000, the French lost 194,000 men and the German losses amounted to 465,000. The result of the battle was indecisive and the war went on for a further two years, the same ground being fought over again during the German spring offensive of 1918.

In the event, German pressure on the French at Verdun meant that the attack would be mainly a

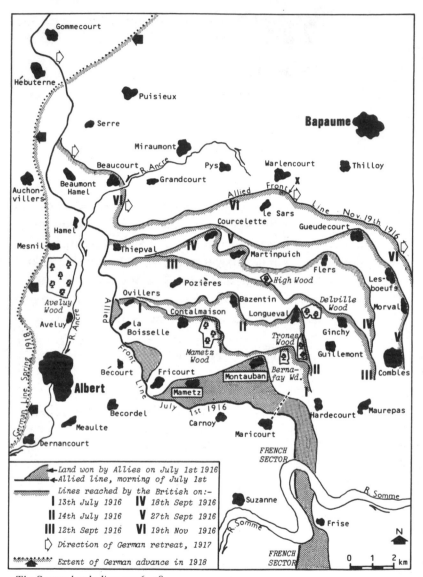

The Somme battle-lines 1916–18

British affair, because a very much smaller French force than the one which had been originally envisaged would take part. If I stress the British role in the battle it is in no way intended to belittle the French army, whose attack mounted astride the River Somme was largely successful.

The British trench lines from which the attack was to be launched stretched roughly for five miles on either side of the Albert to Bapaume road. Just before seven o'clock on the morning of 1 July the men of eighteen divisions (about 100,000 all told) left their trenches and moved towards the German line. They had been told that the five-day artillery barrage which preceded their attack would have destroyed the German wire and so shaken the German defenders that the capture of their positions would be a comparatively simple matter. Things, however, turned out rather differently. High-explosive shells did not destroy the barbed wire, and German machine-gunners, after sheltering in

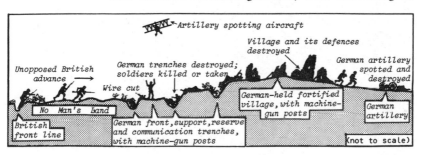

The Somme: *The theory . . .*

. . . the reality

deep dug-outs during the barrage, emerged from them to direct a withering fire at their attackers. By the end of the day the British army had suffered 60,000 casualties, 20,000 of them dead. Gains for this appalling loss were minimal: Mametz and Montauban had been taken, Fricourt isolated. Elsewhere the British line had moved little. After a series of desperate and bloody battles over four and a half months the army had inched forward to a line just beyond Le Sars, Gueudecourt, Lesbœufs, Morval and Combles. Distances and positions can be seen from the map.

Gerald Brenan, who was here in 1916, later described what he saw behind the lines about a fortnight after the battle had started:

> The whole country swarmed with khaki figures, some on carrying parties, others cooking or brewing tea in black dixies, others lying on the ground or sitting up to clean their rifles or rewind their putties. Others again were foraging for firewood or souvenirs or squatting to relieve themselves.[26]

Today the scene of these bitterly fought encounters is quiet and the Somme countryside is sleepy. Only the many memorials and cemeteries bear continuing witness to the conflict.

South to the Somme Battlefields

From Flanders, Loos, Vimy Ridge and Arras travel south to the Somme battlefields, leaving Arras by the D 919. Follow this road to Ayette, where there was heavy fighting during the German offensive of March and April 1918. There is an unusual and interesting Indian/Chinese cemetery in the village. Continue to Bucquoy, which is about 4 km. further

Second Lieutenant, later Captain, J. B. Carson of the Royal Horse Artillery acted as an Intelligence Officer. In this capacity he had a freedom of movement that was denied to officers and men of active units. Even so, he was issued with passes which would be inspected on demand by Military Police patrols active in the back areas

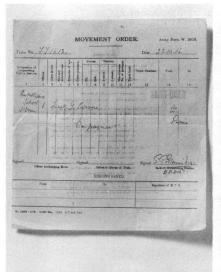

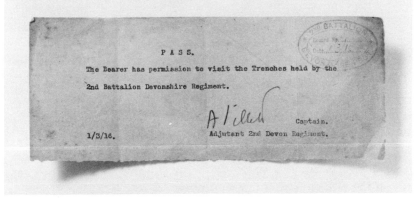

on. Until its capture by the British in March 1917 the village was a German base; and it was from here during the fighting in March 1918 that British Whippet light tanks first went into action.

In the centre of the village turn right on to the D 8 for Hannescamps, 6 km. away. This was always behind the British lines, but was none the less heavily bombarded. Then turn left on to the D 3. Go through Foncquevillers, and from here take the D 6 past Gommecourt Wood and into Gommecourt. On 1 July 1916 the British 3rd Army was involved in fighting here and attacked the village; but having reached the outskirts they did not finally capture it until the end of February 1917. In less than 1 km. take a small road to the right and follow it to Hébuterne, a fortress village in the British front line from which the attack on Gommecourt was also made.

Take the left hand road (D 27) and go to Puisieux, a typical village and one of the many in the area that were reduced to rubble and ruin by repeated bombardment and fighting. Turn right back on to the D 919 for Serre. On the right, a little way out of the village, is the Memorial to the 12th Battalion York and Lancaster Regiment. The road goes on through a number of British and French cemeteries, the legacy of the fighting at the outset of the battle in July. It was in this area that British infantry were mown down by carefully placed German machine-guns, and those who survived were fortunate not to become impaled on barbed wire before they reached the German lines. More cemeteries . . . then Sheffield Memorial Park, a small enclosure up the reverse slope of which British troops had to fight their way in the face of determined opposition. A length of front-line trench and a rear line with shell craters has been preserved here around the Sheffield Memorial. The location can be reached from a track beside the farm at the bottom of the hill.

Back on the D 919, and the largest of the cemeteries is Serre Road No. 2 with 3,300 graves. In 1¼ km., at the crossroads on top of the hill, there once stood a sugar refinery (*sucrerie*), and an important part of the British trench system was here.

Go on to the village of Mailly-Maillet. As you travel, observe the excellent view of Thiepval Ridge to your left. Despite the destruction wreaked in the village, its church still has a fine medieval west door, which escaped harm through the forethought of the local priest, who had it covered up and protected throughout the war.

Take the D 73 for Auchonvillers. One kilometre beyond the village is the Newfoundland Memorial Park. Stop here at the entrance.

Beaumont-Hamel Newfoundland Memorial Park

The park covers more than eighty acres, about half of which formed the sector of the line held by the Royal Newfoundland Regiment on 1 July 1916. In the initial attacks of that morning the regiment was wiped out. At the entrance to the park there is the 29th Division Memorial, and surrounding it you can see the grass-covered trenches of the battlefield. They have been preserved just as they were left in 1918, and the park is one of the best preserved trench memorials on the Western Front. It is dominated by the Caribou monument, at the base of which is the Memorial to the Newfoundland Missing – of whom about 8,000 are listed on the bronze panels. The monument stands upon a plinth of stone around which is an orientation table from which you have an excellent view of the entire park and the countryside beyond to Beaumont and Thiepval. From here, using the orientation table, distinguish the opposing front lines, with the petrified 'Danger Tree' in no-man's land between them. Y-Ravine was a German strongpoint from which machine-guns wreaked havoc upon the opposing infantry. Looking over the ravine is the 51st Highland Division Memorial, with a kilted Scots infantryman looking towards the enemy positions.

It is worth while walking around the battle area. A good deal of battlefield debris still remains in the shell holes: helmets rusting away, shell cases, barbed wire and the iron pickets upon which it was hung. These relics are not there for the taking; they are there to be looked at. Today, some seventy years after the battle, items are still being found, shells and hand grenades are still finding their way to the surface of the well-kept grass, and if anything dangerous is seen it should not be touched, but reported to the Superintendent or to one of the gardeners.

It is in the Superintendent's house in the park that the Newfoundland Roll of Honour is kept. The park itself was taken over in 1959 by the Canadian Battlefield Monuments Commission, and the Commonwealth War Graves Commission provides staff, assisted by a flock of sheep who graze here, to keep it in a beautiful condition.

Leave the park and continue on the road to Hamel. Take the left fork in the village and join the D 50, then after a few hundred metres take the left fork on the D 163E for Beaumont. In the village take the right-hand road, the D 163, for Beaucourt-sur-

l'Ancre. There are several monuments hereabouts
to British units who fought on the Somme, including
one to the 63rd Royal Naval Division. In Beaucourt
rejoin the D 50, turning left towards Miraumont.
Much of the village, used as a German supply base,
was destroyed by British artillery in August 1916.

*The German
enemy on the
Somme*

Then take the D 107, to the right, cross the railway and follow the D 151 right towards Grandcourt, which formed part of the German positions on the River Ancre. Go through the village, take the D 163E to Saint-Pierre-Divion, again part of the German lines. At the junction with the D 73 turn left and go up the hill towards Thiepval. At the top, set in a small park on the left of the road, is the tall, grey Memorial to the 36th Ulster Division. In the fields behind the memorial, during spring and autumn when ploughing is done, traces of the German trenches can be seen. They formed part of a strong defensive position called the Schwaben Redoubt, the site of which is under Mill Road Cemetery.

Thiepval

Continue 1 km. to Thiepval, now a hamlet but once a thriving village. By the end of 1916 it was a ruin. The Germans made it into a fortress, and its capture was vital if the British were to make their breakthrough. The ridge on which Thiepval stands was finally taken by the 51st Highland Division in the late September of 1916, after desperate fighting with heavy losses on both sides.

In Thiepval itself, the great Memorial to the Missing is along the road behind the church, on the right. Designed by Sir Edwin Lutyens, it is built of brick with stone facings. The central archway, flanked by smaller ones, rests on sixteen main pillars. The effect is extraordinary, and the edifice can be seen from miles around. On the monument are recorded the names of 73,412 men who died in 1916–17 and have no known grave. Behind the memorial is a cemetery where equal numbers of unidentified British and French soldiers lie buried. Opposite the memorial is another to the 18th Division. This area is the site of what was once Thiepval Château, and later the Leipzig Redoubt, another strongpoint in the German defences.

At the crossroads in Thiepval there is a small, rather unattractive house that used to be a café. For many years, until her death in the early 1970s, it was owned by a lady named Isobel, who had been there in 1916 and was twice compulsorily evacuated by the Germans when she refused to leave voluntarily. She would on occasion tell customers stories of the war years.

Continue on the D 151 for Authuille. Go through the village, and in about 2 km. turn left on to the D 20. Shortly after this, take a small road on your left leading to Ovillers, which has a large cemetery and overlooks a valley called Mash Valley by British troops. Through the village, taking the right-hand road, brings you to the D 929, the main Albert–Bapaume road. Turn left towards Pozières, which straddles this main road. In 1916 at the outset of the Somme battles it was the focus of heavy fighting, and its ruins were taken towards the end of August by the 1st Australian Division and the 48th British Division of the 5th Army, commanded by General Gough.

Before coming into the village you will pass Pozières Military Cemetery and the Memorial to the Missing of the Fifth Army in 1918. It records 14,690 names.

Pozières*

Go on up the road, which becomes steeper until the

---

* An irony of the fighting in this area was the fact that one German unit, a regiment of Hanoverian Fusiliers, wore a badge with a representation of the Rock of Gibraltar on it. They had been granted this honour some two hundred years earlier, when Britain and Hanover were ruled by the same king.

crest is reached. On either side are the Tank Corps Memorial and the site of Pozièrcs Mill. Around the former are four scale models of Great War tanks, one of which bears bullet marks from the Second World War! It was from this area that the very first tanks were used in an attack on the village of Flers in 1916. The mill is now no more than a grassy mound, but during the war it was Hill 160, a bitterly disputed point. A stone slab on the summit commemorates the Australians who were here in July and August 1916, and it is reached through a memorial gate. The unadorned stone, one of the most moving of all memorials on the Western Front, reads as follows:

> The ruin of Pozières windmill which lies here was the centre of the struggle in this part of the Somme battlefield in July and August 1916. It was captured on August 4th by Australian troops who fell more thickly on this ridge than on any other battlefield of the war.

Further up the road some 1½ km. is the Canadian Memorial of Courcelette, which commemorates a number of actions by the Canadians including their capture of Regina Trench, the longest trench built by the Germans on the Western Front, which ran across the ridge. Turn right on the D 6 for Martinpuich. The village was in ruins long before it was captured by the British half-way through September 1916, and some of the earliest tanks were in action here. The Germans recaptured Martinpuich in March 1918, and it was finally retaken by the British in August.

Continue on the D 6 to Longueval.

Delville Wood and High Wood
All this area saw heavy fighting in both 1916 and

1918, and there are several cemeteries and memorials. When you reach Longueval, take the first road to the right, which leads to Delville Wood and the South African National Memorial. To the south of the road you will see Delville Wood Cemetery. The wood itself (Bois d'Elville in French) is approximately half a mile square and irregular in shape. Half-way through July it was the scene of fierce fighting when the South African Brigade went into action for the first time. One tree situated just behind the memorial, its trunk full of shrapnel, survives from the original wood and is tended by the Commonwealth War Graves Commission. Battle debris, too, can still be found here. The wood has been thoroughly rehabilitated and all the glades have signposts at their junctions, so it is a simple matter to follow the course of the battle that raged here in the latter half of July 1916.

The memorial, a massive triumphal archway, is approached across a lawn between two double rows of South African oak trees.

Go into Longueval village on the D 107; about 1 km. on is the Bois de Fourceaux, better known as High Wood. By the side of the road is a memorial to the 47th (London) Division, which drove the German defenders out of the wood in September 1916.

In a letter signed 'Tommy Atkins', published in the *Sunday Times* on 8 March 1964, an old soldier wrote about his memories of the fighting here:

At High Wood on September 9, 1916, we went in 1,100 strong and at the end of the day only 110 were standing up, with just one officer, a young second-lieutenant, and he was crying: I can remember that roll call now.

One of the German fortified positions can be seen from the road among the trees. On the eastern side of the wood, at the edge of a field, a rather muddy track leads to the Memorial to the Cameron Highlanders and Black Watch, who were fighting here when a large mine was blown. Its crater, now full of water, is on the left beyond the memorial.

The wood itself is privately owned and may not be entered without leave from the owner, who lives in the large house near the road. There are trenches and strongpoints among the trees, and since the area has not been completely cleared of battle debris, trespassing could be dangerous.

Some distance away, on a rise in the ground, the New Zealand Memorial on the site of Crest Farm can be seen. It can be easily reached from the road from Longueval to Flers. Behind it, part of the ground is still cratered from the battle.

Return to Longueval and take the D 197 to Flers, about 4 km. At the end of the main street is the Memorial to the 41st Division. It is surmounted by a bronze infantryman in battle order, his bayonet pointing towards Pozières. This village was the objective of the first tanks that went into action on 15 September 1916. Go on to the next crossroads and turn right to Gueudecourt (another 2 km.), where there was continuous fighting in September 1916. When at last the British army captured it, little was left of the village; and this marked pretty well the furthest point reached by the Allied armies in November 1916 when the battles of that year finally petered out.

Newfoundland Memorial
About $\frac{1}{2}$ km. from Gueudecourt, on the road to

Beaulencourt, is the Newfoundland Memorial, with a caribou similar to that at Beaumont-Hamel. It looks towards the German lines, and stands above a strongpoint within a curve of trenches, and a machine-gun post where the regiment held the line in September 1916.

Continue to Beaulencourt, then turn left on the N 17 for Bapaume.

Bapaume
This quiet market town has a long history dating from Roman times. Because of its situation at a strategic crossroads, it has seen much fighting, and it was a fortified town in the sixteenth century. At the beginning of the war there was fighting here, and then it remained in German hands until March 1917, when it was captured by troops of the 2nd Australian Division. When the Germans left the town they mined or booby-trapped many of the buildings – the Hôtel de Ville was one of these, and it blew up a few days after the Australians had arrived. The Germans reoccupied what was by then a ruined town in March 1918, but were driven out by the New Zealand Division some five months later.

Go through Bapaume and turn left on to the D 929 for Albert. As you ascend the hill in the direction of Le Sars, see to your left a wooded mound. This is the Butte de Warlencourt, an artificial mound that played some part in the Franco-Prussian War of 1871. During the Great War it was somewhat higher than it is today and its possession was hotly contested by both sides. It was not taken by Allied troops until February 1917. The Germans retook it in March 1918, and only in August did

the Butte come finally into Allied hands. On the
crest the base of a German memorial can be seen,
and in the undergrowth beneath the trees some fortified entrances are visible. Hidden in a bush is a
German replacement cross, which was erected in
1944 by a German infantry battalion serving in the
area.

Reaching Le Sars, which straddles the main road,
remember that this was the furthest point reached by
the British on this sector during the Somme battles.
Continue to Albert.

Albert

Albert, once called Ancre, is an industrial town. At
the end of September 1914 it was very nearly taken
by the Germans, but French infantry with British
cavalry in support pushed the invader back, and for
the next two years Albert was just behind the line of
trenches. Because of its proximity to the front it was
always filled with soldiers – at first mostly French,
but in March 1916 the British took over.

The town was frequently bombarded, and on 15
January 1915 a shell toppled the golden virgin from
her plinth on the tower of the Basilica. The statue,
however, did not fall to the ground, but hung rather
precariously, head down, out over the tower. It
caused a good deal of comment, and gave rise to the
legend that, when the 'Leaning Virgin' fell, the war
would end. It was disproved in 1918 after the
Germans' offensive swept them into the town in
March. On 16 April British artillery demolished
the tower with shellfire, and the virgin fell to the
ground . . . Only in August was Albert recaptured
by British forces, and the war ended some three
months later!

Because of the fighting, none of the buildings in Albert is old: the town has been virtually rebuilt. On the Hôtel de Ville there is a memorial to members of the Machine Gun Corps.

In order to form some idea of the ferocity and scale of the fighting during the Somme battles of 1916 it is worth visiting the village of Fricourt (some 5 km. from Albert on the D 938 and D 147). Rising in tiers on the brow of a hill, the village was turned by its German defenders into a series of blockhouses and redoubts with numerous machine-guns. Beneath many of the houses there were deep shelters in which they could escape the worst effects of the prolonged artillery bombardment with which the battle began. Fricourt was also the scene of much underground mine warfare, and the possession of craters was bitterly contested by both sides. Remains of this fighting can be seen on the left of the D 147 where, on the crest of the rising ground, the Tambour Mine and other craters can be seen.

At the outset of the battle the Germans held the village while the French clung rather precariously to its south-western outskirts. After thirty-six hours of incessant fighting the British 17th Division captured Fricourt on 2 July, taking 1,500 prisoners and sustaining many casualties. The dead are buried in Fricourt British Cemetery (where there is a memorial to the 7th Battalion Green Howards) and in Fricourt New Military Cemetery, now surrounded by fields. Both are signposted up in the village.

After the struggle for possession the area was a wilderness, but it was here, in the main street, that an army traffic census was conducted over a twenty-four-hour period about three weeks after the village – or what remained of it – had passed into British hands. The census takers, according to the *Official History*,[27] recorded the following traffic:

Troops	26,536
Guns	63
Cars and buses	663
Motor cycles	617
Lorries	813
6-horse wagons	1,458
4-horse wagons	568
2-horse wagons	1,215
1-horse carts	515
Riding horses	5,404
Motor ambulances	330
Pedal cycles	1,043
Caterpillars	10

More than seventy years later a rebuilt Fricourt dozes in the Somme valley. Standing in its main thoroughfare, it is hard to imagine such an organized mass of men, horses, guns, motor vehicles, carts and

Transport passing through Fricourt during August 1916. It must have been near this spot that the Traffic Census was conducted. Fricourt was known to many in the B E F as the first village on the front to suffer total annihilation

tractors pouring through the ruins on their way to or from the fighting line, which was even then inching towards Bapaume; hard, too, for the imagination to recognize that this was but a typical point in the battle zone – Fricourt was only one of many such villages on the Western Front.

Cambrai

The Battle of Cambrai was fought between 20 November and 5 December 1917. It was conceived as an Allied large-scale raid on the Somme front where the ground was suitable for tanks. Although tanks had previously been in action at Pozières in September 1916, and later during Third Ypres in 1917, their worth in battle was yet to be proved.

Cambrai was to prove a turning point in the history of armoured warfare,* although the battle itself, for reasons unconnected with the use of tanks, was (as ever on the Western Front) indecisive, and casualties were enormous: 44,000 (approximate figure) British and 53,000 German.

The front chosen for the attack was bounded on the east and west by the Saint-Quentin Canal and the Canal du Nord, which were about seven miles apart. The gap was defended by the main Hindenburg position, which consisted of a belt of wire, trenches and interlocking strongpoints about 4,000 yards deep. Behind this there was a second defence line. Supporting the defences was the westward loop of the Saint-Quentin Canal, which turned north again

* The Royal Tank Regiment, direct descendant of the Tank Corps of 1917, very properly celebrates 20 November as its regimental day. This is the anniversary of the first great tank offensive in history.

to Cambrai before it reached the Bourlon Ridge, a dominating spur. Beyond the town of Cambrai the Upper Sensée River ran at right angles to the projected axis of advance. This meant that the British would be attacking into a pocket of land that narrowed, and that river crossings would have to be secured if they were to break through in strength.

On the other hand, the open country for which they would be making did offer the chance for a speedy advance by the tanks, since it was mostly free from the shell craters and mud which had so trapped and impeded these fighting vehicles at Ypres. Moreover, the area was lightly garrisoned.

General J. F. C. Fuller,[28] who was then Tank Corps Staff Officer, chose this front because it offered a chance of success for the tanks. What he had in mind was an enormous raid that would both confuse and demoralize the enemy. General Byng, however – commander of the 3rd Army on whose front the action was to take place – conceived a much more ambitious plan, which included the capture of Cambrai and Bourlon Wood, cutting off German forces between the Sensée and the Canal du Nord, and finally pushing on to Valenciennes. Haig approved this plan with one proviso: if river crossings and seizure of the flanks were not completed within forty-eight hours, the battle was to be called off.[29]

By 19 November there were nineteen divisions on the 3rd Army front. Six infantry divisions had the task of breaking in, and the cavalry corps consisting of five divisions was to exploit the breakthrough. Unusually for Western Front battles, there was to be no preliminary bombardment by artillery – a prelude to battle that invariably alerted the enemy. Four hundred and seventy-six tanks* disposed in three brigades moved up overnight to their positions in ruined villages and the dense thickets of Havrincourt Wood. They had been brought to the rear of the firing line, and as they had moved to their start positions overnight, the sound of their engines was drowned by the noise of low-flying aircraft.

At 6.20 on the morning of 20 November a bombardment began, and simultaneously tanks with infantry in support moved forward. Success was immediate. Within four hours the Hindenburg Line

---

* They had been transported from England via the military port of Richborough in Kent on the train ferry under conditions of great secrecy. A contemporary photograph shows the tanks on board, completely unrecognizable, covered with tarpaulin sheets. They would have covered the seventy or so miles from Calais to the battle area by rail.

was in British hands, except for the village of Flesquières, which was tenaciously defended. It is also true that the commander of the 51st (Highland) Division, which was attacking in this sector, mistrusted the tanks, and kept his infantry too far behind them for much co-operation to be possible.

By evening things looked promising, although not everything that had been hoped for had been achieved. No gap for the cavalry to advance through had yet materialized, Bourlon had not been assaulted, the attacking troops were becoming weary, and 179 of the tanks had been put out of action by enemy fire or mechanical failure. These facts did not prevent the opening stage of the battle from being hailed as a major breakthrough, and on the morning of 21 November church bells were rung in London and elsewhere, for the first and only time before the Armistice, to celebrate a victory that had not in fact been achieved.

The dramatic impact of the tank attack drained away, and German reinforcements were hurried to the line. Had Haig not squandered the lives of so many soldiers in persisting with the Third Battle of Ypres long after it should have been called off, he too would have had divisions in reserve to exploit the initial success. As it was, he had none. The fighting went on, the Germans evacuated Flesquières, and Bourlon became the focus of British attack; but it was stubbornly defended and did not fall. Haig's time limit of forty-eight hours was exceeded, but he was unable to disengage from the fighting round Bourlon; at the same time, through lack of men, he was unable to take advantage of the crossings over the Saint-Quentin Canal held by his men.

On 29 November the Germans launched a surprise attack with some twenty divisions, and regained some of the ground they had initially lost. They also pierced the British front line, and Haig ordered a withdrawal to a line defending pretty well the same amount of ground as the 3rd Army had overrun on the first day of the battle.

I have concentrated upon the Battle of Cambrai because it is the most crucial *historical* engagement of the entire war. Although it was fought largely and traditionally – according to Western Front standards – by the infantry, there is no doubt at all that in the initial stages the tanks had scored a notable success. For the first time the trench deadlock was broken: things, in the long run, would never be the same again.

Third Ypres had demonstrated the folly of continually hurling men against strongpoints and barbed wire – and, indeed, of fighting in a wilderness of mud and rain. Persistence in such folly meant, as we have seen, that Haig was quite unable to exploit the success of a new technology in warfare that might, in the end, have saved lives and perhaps shortened the war.

Six days after the battle had begun, and before the national sense of euphoria occasioned by the successful use of tanks in its initial stages had subsided, Field Marshal Haig, Commander-in-Chief of the BEF, sent a telegram to the firm Wm Foster & Co. Ltd, of Lincoln, expressing his gratitude in the following terms:

The TANKS provided by your Department have rendered very valuable services in the Battle near CAMBRAI. I beg you to accept and convey to all those under you whose skill and labour have produced the Tanks, grateful thanks of the ARMY in FRANCE.

26.11.17   D. HAIG

In their promotional literature produced in the years after the war Fosters described themselves as 'the originators, designers and builders of the famous Fighting Tanks'.

The Cambrai Battlefield

Leave Arras by the D 939, and after about 1 km. cross the railway and take the D 37E to the right, through the centre of Tilloy-lès-Mofflaines. Then proceed out into the country, going through the area of some of the 1917 fighting.

In 8 km. go under the motorway, come into Wancourt and at the church turn right on to the D 33 for Héninel, which is 1½ km. distant. Both these villages were centres of fighting in 1917 and 1918. Turn left and head for Fontaine-lès-Croisilles, turning right at the junction with the D 9. The village is then reached in 1 km. It is on the east bank of the River Sensée. To the right, before crossing the river, you will see a well-preserved German concrete dug-out.

Follow the D 9 to Croisilles and turn left on to the D 5 for Écoust-Saint-Mein. Turn left in the village up the D 10E for Bullecourt, rather less than 2 km. away. This area was much fought over by both Australian and British troops during the Arras battles of 1917. It is also the area where the Hindenburg line, with its deep barbed-wire entanglements, ran across the open countryside. At Bullecourt Church there is a memorial to British and Australian soldiers, which was erected in 1980, and there is also a plaque commemorating the Australians outside the village.

Turn right out of Bullecourt, join the D 38 and follow it to Quéant, about 4 km. away. Turn right on to the D 14 for 3 km. to Lagnicourt-Marcel. You are still where the Hindenburg Line ran, and this part of the line was eventually taken by the 63rd Royal Naval Division. Turn left on to the D 5 for Louverval, some 4½ km. away. At the crossroads with the N 30 is the Cambrai Memorial to the Missing of the battle, and near by is the Louverval Military Cemetery. The walls of the memorial have some excellent bas-reliefs illustrating the Cambrai battles that are well worth looking at.

Make for Hermies straight ahead – the road becomes the D 34 – and come into the village in about 4 km. In 1917, when the 1st ANZAC Corps was here, the village green was a large mine crater.

Follow the D 5 out of the village and over the motorway for 3 km., and you come into Havrincourt. The village is dominated by the château, which was, for a long time, a German HQ. Before the end of the 1917 fighting the village and château were in ruins. Havrincourt was in German hands, on the edge of the battle, but taken by the attackers early in the fighting – and on the edge of Havrincourt Wood there is a memorial to the 62nd Division.

Take the D 15 E/D 92 from Havrincourt to Flesquières, about 3 km. away. There were very heavy German fortifications here, and severe fighting when it was attacked by tanks, many of which were put out of action. In his dispatches on the operations Haig wrote:

Many of the hits upon our tanks at Flesquières were obtained by a German artillery officer who, remaining

'Upsy-Daisy'. Tank 'Hyacinth' of 'H' Battalion, Royal Tank Corps, came to grief in the second German line near Flesquières on the opening day of the Battle of Cambrai, 20 November 1917. The infantrymen in the trench, whose action the tank was supporting, belong to the 1st Battalion Leicestershire Regiment

alone at his battery, served a field gun single-handed until killed at his gun. The great bravery of this officer aroused the admiration of all ranks.[30]

The tanks moving from Havrincourt Wood attacked across these open fields on a 15 km. front; so you are now in tank country.

From Flesquières go over the motorway to Graincourt-lés-Havrincourt, about 2 km. In the village turn right for Anneux, then left on to the D 15. Cross the N 30 and come on to the D 16 for Bourlon – the distance altogether is about 4 km.

To the east of Bourlon is Bourlon Wood, with a Canadian Memorial on the hillside reached by a stepped path between chestnut trees planted in honour of Napoleon. In the undergrowth of the wood there are the remains of a bunker; and here, too, is a Memorial to the Free French of the Second World War.

From Bourlon follow the D 16E for 2½ km. and then turn right on to the D 939. Cambrai is 8 km. further on.

Cambrai

Cambrai has a long history, and is today a bustling and prosperous place. In 1815 the Duke of Wellington was here to receive its surrender after the fall of Napoleon. It was captured by the Germans in 1870, and again in 1914. In 1917 the town was damaged by British bombardment; and even more damage was caused in autumn 1918 by the retreating Germans, who mined many of the buildings as Canadian and British troops successfully advanced upon it from north and south respectively.

The Hôtel de Ville is an impressive building, rebuilt in its former nineteenth-century design after severe damage. In the belfry there are two mechanical figures, 'Martin' and 'Martine', dating from 1510, who emerge whenever the clock strikes the hour.

Happily, two of the original city gates have escaped the turbulence of the past, the Porte de Paris in the south and the Porte Notre-Dame in the north-east. There is a Municipal Museum in the Rue de l'Épée and a cathedral, both of them worth visiting.

About 1 km. out on the D 942, the Rue Solesmes, is the Cambrai East Military Cemetery. Originally German, it was later taken over by the Commonwealth War Graves Commission. The dead of both sides are buried here.

An alternative route from Arras to Cambrai

This is the D 939, a straight road of Roman origin, a distance of about 36½ km.

If you decide to go this way it is worth making a detour to Monchy-le-Preux, about 7 km. from Arras. Turn left on to the D 33 about 1½ km. after going over the motorway and follow the signs into the village. As it was built on high ground, possession of it gave the Germans an excellent view of the Allied positions. It was heavily protected and bitterly contested, eventually falling into British hands in April 1917 in a battle fought during a blizzard.

One of the houses in the village has a bunker in its front garden upon which stands the Newfoundland caribou. Eastward from Monchy stands Infantry Hill, once held by the Royal Newfoundland Regiment. The village was retaken by the Germans in March 1918, and Canadian troops recaptured it in August 1918.

Return to the D 939 and turn left for Cambrai. About 5 km. further on is the village of Vis-en-Artois, which you reach after crossing the River Cojeul. On the upward slope is the Vis-en-Artois Cemetery and Memorial to the Missing. It commemorates those who fell in the 1918 advance in Picardy, and 9,303 names are carved on it. In the cemetery are buried over 2,000 British and Canadian troops who were killed when this sector was captured at the end of August 1918.

Continue to Cambrai.

Verdun and Some American Battlefields

The battles fought by the French army to defend Verdun were among the fiercest and most horrifying of the war. The Germans were determined upon a breakthrough and the French were equally determined that the town should be held. The fighting went on from 21 February to 1 July 1916, and losses on both sides were enormous.

The defence of Verdun was directed by General Pétain, and it was held – although the Germans took some ground and both sides were exhausted by the struggle. The French army in particular had been desperately weakened by the fighting and morale had suffered to a great extent, leading to the mutinies of 1917.

To visit the battlefields today is to realize once more the extraordinary futility of such warfare, and yet again to marvel at the gallantry and endurance of the ordinary soldiers who took part in it. The best place to start from is Reims.

Leave Reims, driving southwards on the N 44, and go to the left on the RD 31 after passing Fort de la Pompelle. Forty-two kilometres from Reims you will reach Suippes, having first crossed a vista of uninterrupted grain fields amongst which are occasional military establishments and cemeteries.

A 'poilu' in mid-winter

Orbeval is 23 km. further on; turn left here on to the N 3 and Sainte-Menehould is 8 km. away. This is an old fortress town that was occupied by the Germans in 1914 and was largely destroyed before it was retaken. Later in the war, during the Argonne fighting, it was a French HQ.

In 9 km. you reach Les Islettes. Turn left here on to the D 2 and it is 10 km. to Le Four-de-Paris. Turn right here on to the D 38 for 5 km., through the Bois de la Gruerie, and note a small road to the left. If you follow it for about a kilometre until it tapers off into a number of muddy tracks you will see a notice reading 'Abri du Kronprinz', and a few yards into the wood is the concrete shelter used by the German Crown Prince Wilhelm. It is now in a very bad state; a good deal of the surrounding wood is cordoned off with barbed wire, and entry to the surviving trenches within is forbidden.

Return to the D 38, turn left and make for Varennes-en-Argonne, 4 km. away.

Varennes

This is remembered today as the town where Louis XVI and Marie Antoinette were arrested before being taken back to Paris and the guillotine. The town now is dominated by the Pennsylvania State Memorial, which commemorates the Americans from that State who died in the fighting here in 1918. The memorial consists of a paved courtyard and central monument surrounded by a double colonnade. In the hillside below are several concrete shelters and bunkers.

The main street of the town is the D 946; to the right is the road to the monument, and a little further on is the Musée d'Argonne, which houses a fascinating local collection, including documents relating to the famous arrest in June 1791. There is also a Museum of Mine Warfare that is unusually interesting.

Keep on the D 946 for Boureuilles, which is about 3½ km. to the south. Turn left there on to the D 212 for Vauquois and the Butte de Vauquois. There was much heavy fighting in this area, and the summit of the hill, which is about 290 m. high, can be reached on foot from a fairly steep path leading up from the car park.

Vauquois

What was once the site of a village on the hilltop is now simply grass, barbed wire and mine craters. There is a memorial here to those who died in the fighting: two extremely good orientation tables on a machine that, for a small fee, will provide you with more detailed explanations in four languages.

Return to the modern village at the bottom of the hill and take the D 38 to the left, leading back to Varennes. Notice, as you come in by this road, the Memorial to the Men of the State of Missouri (one of them who served here and lived to tell the tale was Harry S. Truman). About 6½ km. north of Varennes on the D 946 you come to Apremont.

If you have the time you can make a detour to the left on the D 442 for about 3½ km. There is a German cemetery on the hillside, and a marker on the side of the road indicates a valley down very steep slopes. It was here at the beginning of October 1918 that a battalion of the United States 77th Division were cut off from their comrades for several days.

A further 4½ km. on the D 946 brings you to Fléville. Take the D 4 for 3 km. to Sommerance and

then the D 54/D 123 for Romagne-sous-Mont-
faucon, which is 7½ km. away.

The Meuse–Argonne Cemetery and Memorial
As you approach the town you are driving through
an area where the Americans saw much action. On
the far side of it is the great American cemetery
where 14,000 men lie buried amid the tranquillity of
trees and lawns.

Leave by the Cunel Road (D 123) and in about
3 km. follow the D 15 to the right. Five kilometres
further on you come to Nantillois, and soon the
Butte de Montfaucon comes into view – it is 2 km.
away. The summit of the ridge was known as Hill
336. Once the site of a monastery, a hamlet grew up
here, which was heavily fortified by the Germans;
and today it is the site of the American Memorial.
Steps lead up to the entrance, and there is an observation balcony below the Statue of Liberty from
which there is a superb view of the surrounding
countryside. The hill was captured by the Americans
in late September 1918.

Leave by the D 15, which soon becomes the
D 18. Passing through Malancourt on the way,
continue for a further 5 km., when you can make
another detour if you have time. Turn left on the
D 18A, which leads to Côte 304 with its monument. The quiet scene now is very different from
that during the Great War, when some 19,000 men
lost their lives in this area of hills and woods.

Return to the D 18 and continue for 3 km. to
Esnes-en-Argonne, then take the D 38 on the left
for Chattancourt, 5 km. away. At the approach to
the village take the D 38B on the left for 2 km. or so
and you come to Côte 295. This is the highest ground

in the Forêt du Mort-Homme (Dead Man's Forest), the scene of tunnelling by both sides, but particularly by the Germans – the longest tunnel they made was 3,000 m. long, and others measured from 1,500 to 2,000 m. These tunnels connected the three most prominent hills in the neighbourhood fortified by the Germans.

Return to the main road, the D 38, at Esnes, and continue to Verdun via Charny-sur-Meuse, a distance of some 15 km.

Verdun

An old fortress town, Verdun suffered terrible destruction in the Great War and was badly damaged in the Second World War; but it still retains its air of antiquity. As you would imagine, there are many monuments here recalling the struggles for survival in the past. The town itself was the centre of a circle of forts built on surrounding hills. In their 1914 advance the Germans failed to take Verdun, but the town was close enough to the front line to be often bombarded by their artillery.

In February 1916 the Germans launched their attack on the town. When they did so they had a numerical superiority in men over the French of five to two, and before the assault began the French High Command had given orders for the dismantling of the fortresses so that defence in depth could be organized. The result was that the 'outer parts of the town looked more like an abandoned workshop than a fortress on the watch'.[31]

The scale of the attack – the Germans fired one million shells on the first day alone – took the French by surprise. The railway line to Verdun was cut and the town had to be supplied by road; and eventually

the road from Bar-le-Duc (now called the Voie Sacrée) became the lifeline for the defenders of Verdun. At the outset of the battle the French were badly supplied – they were, to quote Marc Ferro, 'the lost children of 1916'.[32]

Entertainment going on during the bombardment at Verdun

The battle was frightful, and the landscape over which it was fought devastated. Often the French were under fire from their own artillery as they fought desperately and tenaciously to capture or recapture hills and to defend their own positions. There was no established line of defence: improvisation was the order of the day as soldiers clung to their positions in the face of enemy fire.

The fighting also involved increasingly large numbers of men. The French army at this time consisted of some 330 infantry battalions, 259 of which went through Verdun. It was the policy of

General Pétain, who directed the defence, to rotate the fighting troops, and so the constant renewal of infantry and artillery units meant that Verdun became the whole army's battle. Few French colonial battalions took part, and no British.

After the savage fighting in February and early March the battle reached some kind of equilibrium. Wide frontal attacks gave way to local actions, which were short, violent and limited in scope. On 10 April Pétain issued an order of the day: 'Courage,' he wrote, 'we shall win.' In the end, the battle was something less than a victory for the French; but the Germans had failed to break their army, and Verdun was held, and perhaps the French can be

Bruce Bairnsfather was, as this preliminary sketch shows, outstanding in his attention to detail, and his many wartime pictures, funny, moving or serious, depict many facets of life in the B E F (and, occasionally, other armies) with great feeling, vividness and accuracy

forgiven for hailing it as a victory. The price was high, though . . . over 350,000 men had died to save Verdun.

Before undertaking any sightseeing or tours you are advised to visit the Office du Tourisme in the Place de la Nation, across the River Meuse from the Porte Chaussée. From the bridge you come into the Avenue Général Mangin, where you cannot miss the Monument to the Fallen with its five sculpted figures, each one representing five different corps of the French army. They stand shoulder to shoulder above the columns of names. On each side of the monument are fragments from earlier fortifications landscaped into the public gardens. You will see on the wall a memorial plaque to General Mangin.

The Victory Monument towers over the Rue Mazel and the Avenue de la Victoire. In the crypt there are the 'Golden Books', which record the medals awarded to the city.

The Porte du Secours, reached by an avenue of large statues of French marshals and generals, is the entrance to the Citadel. Since Verdun is still an active garrison town, it is a live military installation, and only part of it is open to the public. The walls and ramparts are impressive, but most of the fortress is underground and there are about 4 km. of tunnels. In one of the rooms the selection of the French Unknown Soldier was made from eight bodies – the room can be visited, and so can another that houses a small museum.

There is a rather larger museum in the Hôtel de Ville, a Louis-XIII-style building, rather Italianate in appearance and once a palace.

The cathedral crypt also contains memorials of

the battle. Several pillars represent aspects of it, some depicting the realities and horrors of trench life.

In a town where there are so many statues and memorials there is one that is outstanding. This is the Rodin sculpture in front of the Porte-Saint-Paul in the Place Vauban. It was presented to Verdun by the Dutch people.

Visitors to the town will find many hotels, and there are campsites near by.

Battlefields of Verdun

Two itineraries are recommended.

NOTE: There are many battle sites in this area. The Association Nationale du Souvenir de la Bataille de Verdun et la Sauvegarde de ses Hauts Lieux (ANSBV) has installed boards at clearings in the forest indicating walks and drives to places of interest. The signposting is very good, and places where access is forbidden are clearly marked. A very good map is issued by the Institut Géographique National for the Office National des Forêts. It is called *Forêts de Verdun et du Mort-Homme – Champs de Bataille de Verdun*. The scale is 1:25,000 and the map sheet has translations in English and German. It is readily available in the region.

ITINERARY 1

Leave Verdun driving east on the N 3. On the way you will pass the Cimetière du Faubourg Pavé, a military cemetery where the seven unknown soldiers who were not selected for a symbolic burial have their graves. In 5½ km. turn left on to the D 913, and in about 2 km. take the right-hand fork for Fort de Vaux, which lies 2½ km. further on, up the wooded slopes. Half-way up is a memorial to resistance fighters killed here by the Germans in 1944.

Fort de Vaux

One of the many forts that surround Verdun, this is the north-eastern bastion. As you see it today, it has an air of desolation: time and numerous visitors have laid waste the surrounding area, and the fort itself is now little more than a battered heap of crumbling stone with its iron turrets still visible on the mounds above. Inside, the tunnels through which guides lead visitors are both damp and chill, and one wonders what life for the garrison must have been like, especially under heavy bombardment. After a brave defence the fort was overrun by the Germans in June 1916, and retaken by the French five months later, in November. On one of the outer walls there is a memorial to the pigeon that flew with the last message from the commanding officer, Commandant Raynal.

Return to the D 913 and turn right. In 2 km. you reach the crossroads of Chapelle-Sainte-Fine. The road to your left, the D 112, is the direct route to Verdun, and it goes past several monuments, including a most impressive one to André Maginot, French Minister of War before 1939, who was responsible for the line of forts in northern France bearing his name. He served as a sergeant at Verdun.

At the crossroads itself is the Lion Monument

marking the limit of the German advance, and also commemorating the French 30th Division. Behind the lion, among the trees, can be seen the ruins of Fort de Souville.

Go straight ahead over the crossroads for Fort de Douaumont.

Fort de Douaumont

A short distance further on, on the site of the old railway station at Fleury, is the Mémorial de Verdun. This is a fine museum where the events of the battle are fully explained in admirably designed displays of photographs, documents, military equipment and other relics. Captions are printed in French, English and German, as are the guide books which are available. The displays are set round a life-size section of the battlefield, beneath a large annotated map. While the museum is open films are shown continuously.

Stretcher-bearers and walking wounded at one of the battles for the possession of Verdun

y itself was one of nine villages that were ᴏᴜ___ ᴀted during the fighting. It is marked today only by road name-boards and a chapel.

The Ossuary of Douaumont – largest of the many memorials in the area – can be seen across the trees. It contains the remains of over 130,000 men, both French and German. Another 15,000 bodies who were identified are buried in the cemetery in front of it. The memorial was inaugurated in 1932, and in it there are eighteen sections or chapels, each one dedicated to a different *département* or city in France, with some for the Allied nations. Regular services are held in the chapel, and there is ample car parking. Temporary exhibitions are held from time to time, and from ground-level windows at the rear of the building the bones of unknown soldiers may be viewed. Close by is the Jewish Memorial, which, although smaller, is equally memorable.

Continue to Fort de Douaumont on Hill 388. This was the most important of the ring of forts covering the approaches to Verdun; and with its rough paths, grassy tufts and turrets still remaining, it is very similar to Fort de Vaux. There is an observation post looking out over a panoramic view. To the north of the fort is a military camp, and it is from this direction that the German attack came. Within the fort itself there are guides, although most of them speak only French or German. English-speaking visitors are supplied with translations in typescript.

Another fort near by on the D 913B is the Ouvrage de Froideterre on Côte 345. Roughly 1 km. through the forest is another, the Abri Caverne des Quatre Chemins, on the slope that falls away to the left of the road. All these sites are well signposted with good explanatory notices, plans and orientation tables.

Just beyond the Quatre Chemins complex the road to Froideterre ascends on the right. This village was the scene of action throughout the fighting around Verdun. Along the D 913 and the road to the fort, trees have been cleared to reveal the extent of the shell-torn ground.

Tranchée des Baïonettes
Return to the D 913 and turn left before the Ossuary in order to visit the Tranchée des Baïonettes, situated to the right of the road a little way down the hill. Entry is through a huge gateway with elaborately carved metal doors. After passing a disintegrating monument you can see the concrete canopy and pillars enclosing the trench.

This was a section of front-line trench in which were buried men of the 137th Infantry Regiment as they were moving along it. They were not found until 1919, when a line of rifles with fixed bayonets was seen protruding from the ground. Today only a few are visible, and only seventeen unknown soldiers remain interred here. The other forty who were identified were reburied in Fleury cemetery.

The D 913 now descends gently into the Meuse Valley: Verdun is 6½ km. away.

ITINERARY 2

Take the D 903 out of Verdun and then branch off to the right on the D 964, which follows the valley of the River Meuse. Saint-Mihiel is 34 km. away; and as you go along the road to it you will see signposts to various places of interest including Fort du Troyon, about 2 km. south of Troyon village.

Saint-Mihiel

The Germans captured this town in September 1914, and created the Saint-Mihiel Salient, which remained in their hands until almost exactly four years later, when General Pershing's American First Army, along with French colonial troops, attacked the flanks of the salient. After three days' heavy fighting the town was retaken, with many Germans made prisoner, a good deal of equipment seized and about 200 square miles of enemy-held territory recaptured.

From Saint-Mihiel take the D 907 towards Apremont-la-Forêt and the Forêt de Gobessart. In about 2 km. turn right on a small road that leads to the village of Ailly-sur-Meuse. From here the Memorial to the French VIII Corps can be reached. A path connects it with the Tranchée de la Soif, where concrete bunkers are to be seen, and behind the Memorial in the woods are the remains of an extensive trench system with shelters and bunkers. Since subsidence has made the ground dangerous, the visitor is well advised to keep to the paths.

American Memorial

Go back to the D 907 and turn right for Apremont-la-Forêt. Take the D 12 in the village left towards Montsec, about 7 km. Follow the signs, and a small road to the left ascends the hill and ends in about 1 km. at the steps leading to the American Memorial. It is very prominent in the landscape and provides an excellent vantage point for looking over the area of the Meuse fighting. Within the pillars there are orientation points, together with a large bronze relief map of the area.

Return to the D 12, turning left, then shortly

'Americans in Training'. May 1918. Troops from the 77th American Division, recently landed in France, undergoing instruction from a British sergeant in the Machine Gun Corps. Much of the American battle training was carried out in the back areas

right on to the D 119 in the direction of Richecourt, 4 km. away. Turn left there on to the D 33/D 28 for 6 km. to Essey-et-Maizerais. Cross the D 904 and make for Bouillonville and Thiaucourt-Regniéville (7 km.). Turn left on the D 67 on the outskirts of the town and you will see the Saint-Mihiel American Cemetery.

Saint-Mihiel American Cemetery

Here 4,152 men are buried. The cemetery is dominated by a large eagle sundial, a museum and a chapel. There is also a statue of an American officer in field uniform.

From here you can go straight back to Verdun via Fresnes-en-Woëvre on the D 904.

To return to Reims from Verdun follow the N 3 for 9 km., then turn left when you reach the Voie Sacrée. In 1916 this road to Bar-le-Duc was quite literally the lifeline of Verdun: troops and supplies

came along it to Verdun in an unending stream, and from the town the same lorries brought men who had done their time in the line – and, of course, the many wounded.

A French convoy bringing supplies to Verdun along the Voie Sacrée

The earliest contemporary description of it in English that I have been able to trace is in these words:

> ... those splendid workers, the Territorial soldiers of France, lined the highway on both sides, feeding from their shovels the holes torn by an endless moving chain consisting of thousands of three- and five-ton motor lorries (apart from the necessary swifter vehicles), running no more than sixty yards apart, and running absolutely without check or break, by day or night, to feed the men and guns that saved Verdun and broke the German hopes ...

It may be doubted whether in all the world's history any stretch of road in any country ever sustained such a traffic as that which flowed to and from Verdun during the early months of last year.[33]

During the battle Pétain had his headquarters at Souilly, through which the road passes. Later General Pershing used the town as his headquarters.

Return to the N 3 and turn left. Sainte-Menehould is 36 km. away, and 42 km. further on is Châlons-sur-Marne. Turn right here on to the N 44 for Reims, which is 44 km. away.

Mons

There are several routes to Mons, scene of some of the earliest British engagements with the enemy in 1914 and, ironically enough, of some of the last fighting in 1918. In a military cemetery on the battlefield the first (almost certainly) British soldier to be killed lies in a grave not far from that of the last.

The most direct way is via the A 2 and the A 7/ E 19 motorways, 65 km. from Cambrai to Mons. Another route is direct from Ypres (see p. 200).

Mons

In this modern industrial town bounded on two sides by a coalfield, little or nothing remains of the fighting in August 1914 or November 1918. Neither action was sufficiently prolonged to leave any permanent marks, but there are several memorials in the town, and what is especially worth seeing is the panorama of the battles of Mons. This is to be found in the highest part of the old city, site of the citadel and the old château, in the Belfry. Housing in its tower a carillon of forty-seven bells, the Belfry (built in 1662) is the only one of its kind in Belgium. To enjoy the panorama it is necessary to climb a ladder from the top floor of the tower, which is as far as the lift ascends, but a similar view with a convenient table can be had at the base of the Belfry, from the walls in which it stands.

On the left-hand side of the entrance to the Belfry is the Special Symbol of the Battles of Mons, consisting of earth from the grave of every British soldier who was killed in the battles to which the city gave its name.

In the main square, or Grande Place, the dominant building is the Hôtel de Ville, dating from the fifteenth and seventeenth centuries. The Musée de Guerre is well worth visiting. Centrally situated, it contains what is perhaps the finest collection of relics and memorabilia from both world wars in Belgium. It is worth mentioning, too, that the Mons Tourist Office has produced and has for sale an admirably clear guide to the region. If you are fortunate, you may be able to pick up a copy of the earlier guide by the late Monsieur Georges Licope, the authority on the four battles of Mons: August 1914; November 1918; May 1940; and September 1944.

The Mons Battlefield

The outskirts of Mons have changed enormously over the last fifteen years or so. The advent of SHAPE (Supreme Headquarters, Allied Powers, Europe) at Casteau is one reason for this, but a different kind of industrial life is another important reason – the small establishments have given way to factories, and there has been a considerable revival in canal traffic. New bridges, flyovers and roads have wrought profound changes in the landscape.

Leave Mons by the Chaussée de Bruxelles (the N 6) and come to Nimy in 1 km. This is one of the

older industrial suburbs, and as you go through it
the first of the battlefield tour signs can be seen, as
you pass the town square, at the base of the new
road bridge upon which it is placed.

Take the small road to the right, proceed under
the bridge and go along the narrow road by the
canal bank. A modern bridge spanning the canal is
on the site of the old swing-bridge that was defended
in August 1914 by the Royal Fusiliers. The lock-
keeper's house looks much the same now as it did
then, and marks of battle can be seen at ground
level. Some way further along is the modern railway
bridge, which has replaced the earlier one also
defended by the Royal Fusiliers in the face of the
German advance. On the far side of the canal there
is Nimy Station, where a plaque on the wall commemorates Lieutenant M. J. Dease and Private
S. F. Godley, who won the first Victoria Crosses
awarded in the Great War. Godley, so rumour has
it, was the original of Bruce Bairnsfather's 'Old Bill'
(see footnote, p. 88).

Return to the N 6, bear right after crossing the
bridge (the road is signed 'Bruxelles' and 'SHAPE'),
and go under the motorway. You now come into
Maisières, where the British suffered their first casualties – an event which is commemorated on a plaque
on the church. Over to your left, the great complex
of SHAPE extends over an area which was once as
well wooded as that to your right.*

Five kilometres on, passing the main gates of
SHAPE on your left, go over the crossroads and
come to the village of Casteau. Very nearly on the

---

* Visitors to Mons should be warned. The advent of SHAPE has
made hotel accommodation hard to find unless booked well in advance.

crest of the rise to your left is a stone memorial to
the first contact between British and German forces
at 7 a.m. on 22 August 1914. A mounted patrol led
by Captain C. W. Hornby brushed with a party of
German cavalry, and a Corporal E. Thomas of the
Irish Dragoon Guards fired the first shots by a
British soldier in action on the continent of Europe
for very nearly 100 years.

Across the road from here is the Hôtel Mediers,
upon the wall of which is a bronze plaque recalling
that advance troops of the 116th Canadian Infantry
Battalion were here on 11 November 1918 when the
war came to an end.

Return to the crossroads near SHAPE, take the
left-hand road to Saint-Denis (2½ km.) and turn
right over the motorway to reach Obourg, following
the road and bridge signposted to Mons. At the
south end of the bridge follow the hairpin bend to
Obourg Station. Go over the footbridge across the
railway line, and on the canal bank where the station
once stood is a memorial of red bricks taken from
the old station when it was demolished in 1981,
together with a plaque which had formerly been on
the exterior wall of the waiting room. It commemorates the gallantry of the 4th Battalion The
Middlesex Regiment, which was in action here on
23 August 1914.

Go back over the bridge towards Obourg, turning
left on to the road beneath it. Drive along to the
right by the canal, about 4 km., to Ville-sur-Haine.
At the junction with the N 538 turn right into the
Rue de Mons. In Havré village, near the ruins of
the old château, turn left on the Villers-Saint-
Ghislain road. At the N 90 junction, 4½ km.
further on, turn right, then first left for Harmignies.

Just over 1 km. to the right there are two plaques in a field which commemorate the first crash by a Royal Flying Corps aircraft on active service on 23 August 1914.

This road gives excellent panoramic views over the ground where the British and Germans clashed. It soon drops down to Harmignies where the Royal Horse Artillery were based. At the major crossroads in the village turn left on to the N 40 and drive to Givry, $3\frac{1}{2}$ km. It was here that 1 Corps, commanded by Sir Douglas Haig (later to become Commander-in-Chief), faced the Germans immediately before the retreat from Mons began.

Turn left on to the N 563 at the next crossroads, follow the straight road 10 km. for Waudrez. Turn left on to the N 90, then take the first right on to the N 27, which climbs over a ridge before descending to Péronnes. About 200 m. along this road on the left is a water tower opposite a factory. This provides an excellent vantage point from which to look at the ground the BEF fought over in 1914, when the war was one of movement and had not solidified into the static trench positions of 1915 onwards. It was in the fields about here that 'E' Battery of the Royal Horse Artillery went into action – the first time British heavy guns were fired during the war. If you look closely on the right side of the road about 3 m. from the pavement outside the factory, a small stone, almost hidden, commemorates this happening. The gun which fired the shots is today in the Imperial War Museum in London.

Return to the N 90 and make for Villers-Saint-Ghislain, about 5 km. away. Go through the village, where General Allenby once had his headquarters – the red-brick house on the left of the road, where the schoolmistress lived, looks much the same now as it did then.

Saint-Symphorien Cemetery

Two kilometres outside the village turn left at the signpost. In many ways this is the most striking of all the British cemeteries on the Western Front. Its layout is that of a traditional English garden with flowers, shrubs, trees and shady paths. Originally this was a German cemetery, and here they buried their own casualties of the August 1914 fighting, and the British dead as well. They erected a number of memorials here, one dedicated to the 'Royal Middlesex Regiment';* another is an obelisk to the dead of both sides in the fighting of 23 and 24 August 1914.

The former memorial can be found by taking the path to the right as you enter, and is on the left a little way up. Close by is the headstone of Private J. Parr, The Middlesex Regiment, almost certainly the first man of the BEF to be killed. He died in the evening of 21 August, having failed to return from a scouting mission on his bicycle. Opposite is the grave of the last man to die, on 11 November 1918, Private G. E. Ellison of the Royal Irish Lancers.

Other memorials are worth seeking out here, and the German part of the cemetery differs markedly from the British one – the markers are of grey granite, and those of the officers are more flamboyant in style than those of the non-commissioned officers and privates.

Go back to the entrance, which borders on a new housing estate. Driving back the way you came, take

---

* An error on the part of the Germans. The Middlesex Regiment was never royal.

the first left, then the first right on to the N 90,
over the crossroads at La Bascule, where there was
heavy fighting. On the corner there is a memorial to
the Royal Irish Regiment. Remaining on the N 90,
return to Mons.

From Ypres to Mons

Take the N 8 from Ypres to Menin (Menen), 18
km. away. This industrial town was an important
German base and supply depot for troops fighting around Ypres. It was not finally taken by the
Allies until October 1918. To the north, beside the
road to Moorsele, is the Menin German cemetery,
where more than 48,000 bodies are buried.

Continue on the N 8 to Courtrai (Kortrijk), also
a German army base. Like Menin, it fell to the
Allies in October 1918. During the Second World
War the town was damaged in air raids; but happily
one of its older fortifications, the Broelen Toren,
survived the bombing. This is a bridge over the
River Leie (Lys) with two great towers, one of them
now a museum.

Follow the N 50 to Tournai (Doornik), about
27 km. distant. For the last 10 km. the road follows
the course of the River Schelde (Escaut). At
Esquelmes, about 7 km. from Tournai, there is a
little churchyard on the river bank in which there
are some war graves dating from the last months
of the fighting. In the fields about 1 km. along a
narrow road running parallel with the canal is a
1939–45 cemetery containing the graves of men
killed in 1940.

Come into Tournai along an avenue of very fine
trees. The cathedral with its five towers dominates
the centre of the city, and a marvellous view of the

surrounding countryside can be had from the gallery near the top of the Belfry in the Grande Place.

Until 1830 Tournai was a French city, and the scene of much warfare. From 1513 to 1519 it was occupied by English soldiers* while Henry VIII attempted to integrate Tournai with England. During the occupation the city's fortifications were improved. A survivor from those times is the Henry VIII Tower, a solid two-storey building that now houses a small but interesting collection of weapons of war from several centuries.

Tournai during the Great War was another important German base. The British army entered it on 8 November 1918, finding the bridges and many buildings destroyed.

Leave Tournai eastwards on the N 7, and at Warchin join the E 42 autoroute. After about 30 km. take the A 7/E 19, and after 11 km. leave the motorway at the Mons-Jemappes exit. Turn left on to the N 550 and in 2 km. come into Mons.

For the Mons Battlefield, see p. 195.

---

* See C. G. Cruikshank, *The English Occupation of Tournai*, 1513–19 OUP, 1971. It is worth recalling, too, that the Duke of Marlborough's army fought over this area. Oudenarde and Malplaquet, scenes of battles in 1708 and 1709, are not far away. See David Chandler, *The Art of Warfare in the Age of Marlborough*, Batsford, 1976.

South from Mons

(to Le Cateau, Saint-Quentin and Amiens)

Mons to Le Cateau

The road south from Mons is pretty well the route followed by the retreating British army in 1914, and much the same as that followed by advancing Allied troops in the autumn of 1918.

Take the N 6 from Mons, and in $3\frac{1}{2}$ km., at Ciply, take the right fork, the N 543. Go through Noirchain, $3\frac{1}{2}$ km. away, to Blaregnies, some 6 km. further on. Within 2–3 km. you reach the Franco–Belgian frontier, and here the road becomes the D 932. Look on the left shortly after crossing into France for the site of Malplaquet, a battle fought by the Duke of Marlborough's army in 1709.

Eight kilometres on from the border you come to Bavay, where, in the Mairie, or town hall, General French had his Advanced Headquarters during the Battle of Mons in 1914. Take the D 942 for Le Quesnoy, 14 km. away.

Le Quesnoy

Le Quesnoy is an old town that has preserved its seventeenth-century ramparts and is still largely enclosed within them. On 25 August 1914 the BEF retreated south from here on roads which were

choked with refugees. For the next fo
remained a German garrison town, un
successfully assaulted by the New Zealand ..vision
in early November 1918.

The D 33 leads to Jolimetz, $4\frac{1}{2}$ km. away, where
you rejoin the D 932 on the western edge of the
Forest of Mormal, a large woodland of about 22,000
acres that covers the high ground and the slopes
between Bavay and Landrecies. In 1914 the route of
the advancing German army lay through the forest,
and four years later Allied soldiers passed through it
as they pursued the retreating Germans.

As you meet the D 932 turn right towards Engle-
fontaine, 5 km. off. Turn left here on to the D 934
and reach Landrecies in 9 km. As the British troops
were retreating in August 1914 a brisk rearguard
action was fought in the streets here. The town fell
into German hands, and was not recaptured until
one week before the Armistice.

From Landrecies take the D 959 through Bois
l'Évêque, where there was fighting in 1914 and 1918.
Turn left after 4 km. to Ors. There is a British
Communal Cemetery by the station, and here
Wilfred Owen, one of the outstanding poets of the
Great War, is buried. Continue on the D 160A and
join the N 43 for Le Cateau.

Le Cateau

A town known to most members of the original
BEF, Le Cateau was the first site of British General
Headquarters, and there was a battle here on 26
August 1914 – the site can be visited from tracks
leading off the D 932 or the D 21.

A cenotaph set within a grove of trees commemorates the Suffolk Regiment, the Manchester

Regiment, the Argyll and Sutherland Highlanders, and their artillery support.

As you come into Le Cateau from Landrecies there is a crossroads with the Hôtellerie du Marché (Market Hotel) on the corner. Near it you will see a horse trough, now used to display flowers, which is the Memorial of the British 66th Division, who, together with a South African Brigade, drove the Germans out of the town in August 1918.

Half-way up the main street – which, like many others in the town, is cobbled – stands the Hôtel de Ville with its entrance under the central tower. In the foyer and up the staircase to the library and museum are pictures by Henri Matisse, who was born here.

Some 150 British soldiers are buried in the town cemetery, where there is a German memorial to all the combatants. The British Military Cemetery lies just north of the D 932 and N 43 crossroads. Beside the graves of British and German soldiers are buried a small number of Russians, and there are several memorials. The German section, which has a separate entrance, has recently been considerably tidied up by the German War Graves Authority.

Le Cateau to Saint-Quentin

Leave Le Cateau on the D 932 and drive about 23 km., then turn right on the D 93. Go through Nauroy, and Bellicourt is 2 km. away. The Saint-Quentin Canal emerges from a tunnel south of the village; and directly above it, on the heights, is the Bellicourt Monument, which recalls American troops who fought in this area in 1918. On the west face of the monument is a map showing the operations of the two American divisions who were here, and there is a useful orientation table.

The canal tunnel here was used by the Germans as part of their defensive system called the Hindenburg Line, and there was heavy fighting at its northern end in September and October 1918 when British and American troops successfully breached the defences. Today there is little sign of war either in the tunnel or on the banks of the canal.

About 3 km. to the north on the N 44 is the Somme American Cemetery at Bony. Either from here or from Bellicourt, go south on the N 44 towards Saint-Quentin. On the way you will pass through Riqueval, the southern end of the canal tunnel just referred to. It is easily reached from the road, and near it is a memorial to the soldiers from Tennessee who were killed here in the canal battles. Saint-Quentin is 11 km. from here.

Saint-Quentin

An industrial city on the banks of the Somme, Saint-Quentin was held by the Germans from the end of August 1914 until October 1918 (R. C. Sherriff's famous war play *Journey's End* was set in 'A dugout in the British trenches before Saint-Quentin'). Today little trace of the war is to be seen. In the cathedral, in one or two pillars, there are bore holes drilled by the Germans to take demolition charges. Fortunately the cathedral was not blown up, though it was badly burned. Near the railway station there is a large French memorial upon which are depicted, in bas-relief, various aspects of army life.

Saint-Quentin to Amiens

There are several interesting routes: the one I suggest is via Péronne and Villers-Bretonneux.

Travelling west, leave Saint-Quentin on the N 29, passing through Francilly-Selency in some 4 km.

and Vermand in seven more. This small town was totally destroyed in March 1917 during the German retreat, and was the scene of fighting in the following year. Seven kilometres further on, at Estrées-en-Chaussée, turn right on to the D 44 for Péronne, 10 km. distant.

Péronne

Péronne is a very old town situated at the junction of the Somme and the Cologne rivers. The Germans occupied it in 1914 and used it as a base. About 2 km. to the north is Mont-Saint-Quentin, which was developed by the Germans into a formidable fortress that withstood the French advance on the Somme in 1916 in support of the British offensive. The Germans evacuated the hill in 1917, but took it back a year later. At the end of August 1918 both Mont-Saint-Quentin and Péronne fell to Australian troops during their advance. The town was laid waste during the fighting, but has been completely rebuilt.

At the time of writing – March 1988 – there are reports of a Somme museum being created in the town. It is to be called the Historial de la Grande Guerre and will stress the British role in the battle.

Driving south, leave Péronne on the N 17, and after about 7 km. turn right on to the N 29. Go through Villers-Carbonnel almost immediately, then along this straight road come to Villers-Bretonneux in about 27 km.

Villers-Bretonneux

There is a demarcation stone near the approaches to this small agricultural and industrial town where most of the buildings lie to the south of the road.

THE LONG AND THE SHORT OF IT

UP LAST DRAFT: "I suppose you 'as to be careful 'ow
you looks over the parapet about 'ere"
OUT SINCE MONS: "You needn't worry, me lad; the
rats are going to be your only trouble"

Before April 1918 it was behind the British lines, and on its outskirts was a Royal Flying Corps aerodrome. The town was taken by the Germans, using tanks in support of their infantry, on 24 April 1918 and recaptured by the Australians on the following day. During the next four months both sides settled down (if that is the phrase) to static warfare and the opposing armies dug themselves in; but on 8 August Australian and Canadian troops overwhelmed the Germans, the battle rolled forward, and Villers-Bretonneux was once more well behind the fighting line. Casualties, however, had been high. Captain John Hayward of the Royal Army Medical Corps, a surgeon attached to a Casualty Clearing Station, witnessed the start of the August fighting and recalled the arrival of the wounded:

On that evening the attack began, with a continuous roar of heavy guns, while the horizon was brilliantly lit with the flashes of exploding dumps, Verey lights and star shells. The camp was quietly resting, and I was left with a few orderlies in the dimly lit reception tent. About 1 a.m. the ambulances began to arrive.

It is impossible to convey an adequate picture of the scene. Into the tent are borne on stretchers, or come wearily stumbling, figures in khaki, wrapped in blankets or coats, bandaged or splinted. All of them stiff with mud, or caked with blood and dust, and salt sweat, and with labels of their injuries attached. They come in such numbers that the tent is soon filled, and what can be done? I can't cope with them all! Many are white and cold, and lie still and make no response, and those who do are laconic, or point to their label . . .

It was extraordinary that in this charnel tent of pain and misery there was silence, and no outward expression of moans or groans or complaints. The badly shocked had passed beyond it; others appeared numbed, or too tired to complain, or so exhausted that they slept as they stood. Even the badly wounded often asked for a smoke . . .[34]

To reach the Australian National War Memorial and the British Cemetery, take the D 23 to the right in the direction of Corbie for about 2 km. uphill. From the top of the tower that dominates the scene, and has an orientation table, there is a fine view of the surrounding countryside and the battle area where, in spring and autumn, traces of old trenches can be seen as chalk slicks in the brown well-filled fields. To the west, on a clear day, the spire of Amiens cathedral can be seen.

Every year on ANZAC day, 25 April, a special service to mark the Australian role in the battle for the town is held at the memorial, and there are celebrations in the town. Another link with Australia is the Sir William Leggatt Museum, housed in the school buildings and opened in 1975, providing a good record of the role played by Australians and French in the fighting. Access to the museum, which was a gift from Australian children to those of Villers-Bretonneux, can be obtained by application to the Hôtel de Ville.

Continue on the N 29 towards Amiens, 17 km. away.

Amiens

Amiens, capital of Picardy, has a history of contact with England going back over 400 years. It was here in 1802 that the Peace of Amiens was signed, bringing a brief respite in the war against the newly born French republic, and then Napoleon.

In August 1914 it was the base for soldiers arriving from Britain; but this arrangement was short-lived, as the town was occupied on 30 August by the Germans. They held it for twelve days before being driven out by the French, who kept a garrison there until 1916, when the British took over. It became an important supply, medical and recreational centre for the BEF, with trains from Le Havre bringing in both men and supplies and taking away the wounded. In 1918, for a time, Amiens came within range of heavy German guns; but it was much more seriously damaged in the Second World War, so that today it is essentially a city of modern buildings.

There is a fine cathedral with a number of Great War memorials in it, and the Picardy Museum in the town centre contains material relating to the history of the city, besides a large art gallery.

Amiens is a good centre for visiting the Somme battlefields. The D 929 goes straight to Albert, which is 28 km. away.

Reims to Compiègne

Take the RD 380 south-west out of the city and in 17 km. or so, around the village of Bligny, you are in an area where the British were fighting in June and July 1918. If you have time, take the RD 386 to the left through the village for Marfaux, 5 km. away, where there is a Memorial to the New Zealand Missing and a small British cemetery.

Return to the RD 380, turn left and ascend towards Chambrecy. On the crest of the hill there is an Italian Memorial Garden to your right and an Italian cemetery to your left. The road now descends steeply, and at the bottom there is a British cemetery.

Two kilometres further on, come into Ville-en-Tardenois, which was strongly defended by the British in June 1918. After another 4½ km. turn right on to the D 2, passing through the villages of Goussancourt, 3½ km. away, and Coulonges-Cohan, a further 8 km. distant. Stay on the D 2, and about 5 km. further on is Nesles, and just beyond it on the right the Oise–Aisne American Cemetery.

Oise–Aisne American Cemetery

Over 6,000 men are buried here, and in the chapel are recorded the names of 241 men who have no known graves. The memorial is impressive, with 36½ acres bordered with clumps of trees. There is a car park and a map room that explains the 1918 fighting in this area.

Fère-en-Tardenois is 2½ km. further on. From 12 September to 8 October 1914 British General Headquarters was situated here. The Germans captured it in May 1918 and it was retaken by the Allies two months later.

Turn left in the town on to the D 967 towards Château-Thierry, 22 km. distant.

Château-Thierry

It was here at the beginning of September 1914, during the first British offensive of the war, that men of 1 Corps BEF crossed the River Marne. The town remained in Allied hands until May 1918 when it was taken by the enemy, to be recaptured by American troops some two months later. This was the Americans' first offensive, and the town is today dominated by their memorial. To reach it leave town going west by the N 3 and ascend a fairly steep hill for about 3 km.

American Memorial

The entrance to the memorial is on a corner, to your left, marked by two steep pylons. From here it is about 1½ km. to the memorial itself, which is enormous. It consists of a double colonnade above a terrace within an arc of trees. On the west are two figures representing France and the USA; and on the east a vast eagle is perched over a map of the area in which the Americans fought. An orientation table is on the floor of the terrace.

Come back to the main road and cross it to

join the D 9 for the village of Belleau, 8 km. distant.

Belleau, the American Cemetery and Belleau Wood

Down the village street there is a drinking trough filled with flowers, a gift to Belleau from the Belleau Wood Memorial Association in memory of Pennsylvanian soldiers who were killed in the fighting here. At the bottom of the street are the château stables where American soldiers were billeted. Outside the reconstructed church is a Demarcation Stone; and within it – a key is held by the Cemetery Superintendent – are some commemorative stained-glass windows, together with memorials and the flags of some American units.

Opposite is the entrance to the cemetery, where 2,288 men lie buried. On the walls of the chapel, which has an imposing tower, are inscribed the names of 1,060 men who have no known graves. There is an observation platform in the tower, and from it there is a splendid view of the surrounding countryside. Near by is a German cemetery where 8,625 men have their graves.

To visit Belleau Wood turn right from the cemetery, then take the first right and the first right again to enter the wood. A road ascends to its centre, where there is a flagpole and a Memorial to the 4th US Marine Brigade, which captured Belleau Wood on 25 June 1918 after hard fighting. Amongst the trees are various guns and mortars captured by the marines. There are traces – no more – of both trenches and craters if you look carefully. In a glade towards the cemetery there is a ruined chapel bearing a plaque commemorating the 2nd Division.

Leave the wood by the road to Lucy-le-Bocage. Beyond the village, cross the N 3, which is about 1 km. away, and follow the D 82 for Coupru, about another 1½ km. Shortly the road becomes the D 11. Continue along it, passing through Domptin, for Charly, 7½ km. away from Coupru. Turn right here on to the D 969. The countryside is beautiful, and in 8 km. you reach Luzancy. Close to the entrance to this village is the site of a weir that British infantry used to cross the River Marne in 1914 when the bridge had been blown up.

Seven kilometres away is La Ferté-sous-Jouarre, which was the scene of action by the British army in 1914.

La Ferté-sous-Jouarre

The Germans were well dug in on the northern banks of the river, and the bridges were destroyed. To enable the left wing of the BEF to cross, the Royal Engineers built a pontoon bridge. This temporary crossing, the position of which is now marked on each bank by columns surmounted by Royal Engineers insignia, is close to the modern bridge on the main Paris road. At its southern end is the British Memorial to the Missing on which the names of 3,888 men killed in the 1914 battles of Mons, Le Cateau, the Marne and the Aisne are inscribed.

Leave the town on the N 3 (the main road to Paris, which is 65 km. from here). In 20 km. you reach Meaux, which the BEF entered on 3 September 1914. After some action they moved to the Forest of Crécy, 18 km. to the south, and it was from here that their great retreat began.

From Meaux go northwards by turning right on to the D 405. In about 1½ km., as the road climbs out of the town, there is a park to the right, which is dominated by a vast piece of sculpture, the American Memorial to the French Combatants of the Marne. One kilometre further on turn left on an un-numbered road for Chambry, and at the outskirts of the village turn left on to the D 140 for 1 km., then right on to the D 38 at the crossroads. Here is the Monument des Quatre Routes.

You will now be travelling through the area held by the French 6th Army in 1914 and reinforced by 11,000 soldiers from Paris who were brought to the battlefront in taxis – the so-called 'taxis of the Marne'. Twenty-one kilometres further on is the town of Betz, and on the plateau as you approach it is one of the memorials to the 'Army of Paris'.

From Betz take the D 332 for Crépy-en-Valois, 10 km. away. Turn left here on to the N 324 for $2\frac{1}{2}$ km., then right on the D 25 for Rocquemont. From this village travel north-west, join the D 98 at Verrines, continue to the junction with the D 113 and turn right for Néry, altogether about 4 km.

Néry

The church in this village is close to where a battery of the Royal Horse Artillery, and later the 1st Battalions of the Middlesex Regiment and Scottish Rifles, fought a brief but successful rearguard action with the Germans in the course of which the gunners won three Victoria Crosses. The field guns were situated behind the church, a position which is now overrun by shrubs. The nearby farm, however, probably looks much the same now as it did then.

Continue to Vaucelles on the D 98, about 3 km., then join the D 123, travelling east, for Elincourt, about 9 km. distant. Turn left here on to the D 335 towards Pierrefonds, 9½ km. away. As you approach the town, the castle, looking like something out of a fairy-tale, comes into view. Reconstructed in the nineteenth century under the direction of Viollet-le-Duc, it is said to be the most outstanding example of his work. Go through the town on the D 335. Seven kilometres further on turn left on to the N 31. In 7 km. turn right at the sign 'Clairière de l'Armistice'.

Clairière de l'Armistice

The Armistice was signed here on 11 November 1918.

Delegates from Germany had arrived by train at seven in the morning of 8 November: Erzberger, Secretary of State; Count Obendorff, a diplomat; General von Winterfeldt from the army; Captain Vanselow of the navy. The train that Marshal Foch was using as his headquarters was already waiting in a siding about a hundred yards away, and from it came General Weygand to inform the Germans that the Allied Commander-in-Chief would see them at nine o'clock precisely.

At that hour they entered the railway carriage where negotiations were to take place. The atmosphere was icy. The German delegates were received with formal courtesy by General Weygand and Admiral Sir George Hope, and the French general said he would inform Marshal Foch of their arrival. Almost immediately Foch, accompanied by Sir Rosslyn Wemyss, entered the carriage, asked the names of the German delegates and formally requested their credentials. When the necessary documents were produced he retired with Wemyss to examine them; and on his return Foch invited

Erzberger to introduce the other members of the delegation, and then presented the members of his own mission.

Formalities were over. The two sides faced each other across a narrow table, and Foch asked the Germans what they wanted. To all inquiries about any Allied proposals, any conditions under which an armistice might take place, he remained brusque and blunt: he had no proposals, no conditions to discuss, no concessions to offer. Germany, Erzberger said, was starving, law and order had broken down, the army no longer obeyed orders . . . Foch cut his words short: 'You are suffering from a disease of the vanquished.'

The ghost of the French defeat at German hands in 1870 had been laid. When eventually the Allied terms – harsh terms – were read out, the Germans retired to consider them. Their request for a suspension of hostilities had been peremptorily refused; and in fact, after this first meeting Foch issued what was to be the last General Operation to the effect that the enemy was on the run and that offensive operations must be maintained and intensified.

On the night of 10/11 November there was another meeting. It ended at 5.15 in the morning, when the armistice document was signed. News of the cease-fire was sent to all units, and the war ended at 11 a.m.

After the war, the marshy spot where this took place underwent a transformation and became a national memorial called the Glade of the Armistice, opened in 1932. In the meantime the coach used by Foch and the others (Wagons-Lits-Company No. 241 9D) had been returned to normal railway service;

but it was later exhibited at Les Invalides in Paris, where it attracted many visitors. In 1927 it was refurbished to look as it had done nine years earlier, returned to the clearing in the forest and housed in a specially built shed.

In June 1940, after the fall of France, Hitler received the French surrender at the identical spot in the same coach – which was then put on display in Berlin and disappeared towards the end of the war. The *carrefour* was repaired and a new shed was built to replace the one destroyed during the occupation; and on 11 November 1950 a copy of the original coach, complete with replica furniture and fittings and facsimile documents, was run into the shed. It has since proved to hold as much interest for visitors as its genuine predecessor.

Amiens to Calais

A Lost Landscape of Supply

The route from Amiens to Calais is away from the
fighting line, although it is, in part at least, the route
by which soldiers and supplies came to the Western
Front. Those destined for the battlefields of
Flanders went, roughly speaking, to the area around
Poperinge. No great distances, once a French port
had been reached, were involved in the transport of
men and supplies for the BEF; but as the war went
on the sheer quantity of material, to say nothing of
manpower, became ever greater, and the organization for dealing with it increasingly complex.

Behind the fighting lines, as we saw around
Poperinge, there grew up a litter of bases, depots,
dumps, hospitals, training camps, reinforcement
holding units, vehicle parks, remount depots and so
on . . . the army even ran its own prison at Blargies,
near Rouen. Then there was a constant coming
and going of men – reinforcements, leave men,
wounded, men going on courses to learn about new
techniques and new weapons. Much – indeed, most
– of this movement was by train, although lorries
and motor ambulances were being used in ever

'What the 'ell are you doin', spinnin' a web?'
'Nao! My puttee's undone, sargint'

creasing numbers. A tremendous effort went into
keeping the army supplied and serviced, and it was

absolutely vital to the continuing existence, well-being and eventual success of the BEF. If today we recall primarily the fighting soldiers, and the stretcher-bearers and doctors who tended them, we should also spare a thought for those who took part in this servicing activity.

It was, for instance, usual for every static unit to announce itself by means of a large painted sign at the main entrance. A sign – such as 'Number 4 Remount Depot RAVC' – would serve to identify and locate specific support or supply units.* But it has to be said that some officers attached an exaggerated importance to these manifestations of identity, and also to the quality of this directional information in their own camps. At a time when sign-writers were in short supply, they would go to unusual lengths to secure one.

A story is told (and it is one that will have a ring of truth to anyone who has served in the ranks of the army) of a Field Ambulance stretcher-bearer who reported sick with toothache. He was sent down the line to a Casualty Clearing Station where there was a dentist. In civilian life the stretcher-bearer had been an artist; but while in the Casualty Clearing Station, feeling that he would like a break from the front line, he let it be known that he was a sign-writer (he had never painted a sign in his life!), and that he did not think much of the quality of the unit signs. The regimental sergeant-major heard about this and went to the colonel – who was immediately impressed:

'Keep him here till he's sign-written the whole place,' he

---

* Front-line signs tended to be much more rough and ready. There is a good collection of them in the Imperial War Museum in London.

told the R S M. 'Mark him "Scabies". Give him beer for
breakfast and beer for supper, but hold him till every
sign looks as though it had been painted by an Old
Master!'

So the stretcher-bearer spent three happy weeks
painting signs at his leisure, and eventually went
back to his unit at the front.[35]

The problem of getting food to men in battle was
very much the 'sharp end' of the supply process,
and responsibility for it lay with the quartermaster-
sergeant. There was an episode during the Third
Battle of Ypres in 1917:

> There were four Company Quartermaster Sergeants,
> myself and three others, and we decided between us that
> two of us should go forward to try to find the battalion,
> one would stay with the rations, and the other one would
> try to find the Brigade Headquarters to get some indi-
> cation as to where the battalion might be. We tossed up
> for the different jobs and it fell to my lot to have to find
> Brigade Headquarters, so I set off. There was a most
> tremendous bombardment going on all the while. After a
> while I found the Brigade Headquarters. They were in an
> underground German pillbox just in front of Saint-Julien
> [St Juliaan]. I went down the stairs, saluted the Brigadier,
> told him who I was, explained the position and said,
> 'Could you give me any instructions, Sir, that would help
> me to find the battalion?'
> He just stood and looked at me. We were both standing
> on the steps, and the pillbox was rocking like a boat in a
> rough sea with explosions. After a while he said, 'I'm
> sorry, Quarters, I'm afraid there isn't any Hertfordshire
> Regiment.'[36]

Ultimately the 600 rations, together with rum,
destined for the battalion that had ceased to exist,
were distributed to any men they could find; and

then the ration party returned five or six miles through the mud and rain to their transport lines.

After so many years visible evidence of all this vast activity has all but disappeared. Little of the Calais that the BEF knew as a major base remains. To look today for this landscape of supply is to look in vain; but the accounts left to us by those who were there help us to imagine it.

Leave Amiens by the N 235 to Picquigny, 13 km. to the north-west, then join the N 1. Abbeville (via Flixecourt) is 34 km. on.

Abbeville

In August and September 1914 some German advance parties entered the town, but by the end of the latter month it was firmly held by the Allies, and remained so for the years of the war. There was fighting here in 1940, when a French division commanded by General Charles de Gaulle clashed with German forces that had crossed the river. Because so much of the old town was destroyed by enemy bombing in 1940, little remains today of the town as it was during the Great War; but it was then an important British base and supply centre.

From Abbeville there is a direct route following the N 1 to Montreuil, but the alternative one via Hesdin is more interesting.

To Montreuil via Hesdin

Leave Abbeville on the D 928, and in 16 km. you reach the village of Fontaine-sur-Maye. Turn left at the crossroads on to the D 56, and in $2\frac{1}{2}$ km. there is an old cross mounted upon a modern plinth marking the death of John of Bohemia at the Battle of Crécy in 1346. The cross, which was erected after the battle, is said to be one of the oldest battle monuments in France. The small town of Crécy-en-Ponthieu is 2 km. further on, and in its centre is another old monument, with an inscription in English relating to Eleanor of Aquitaine. Leave the town on the D 111, driving northwards, and notice on the right a transformer hut that marks the site of a windmill from which King Edward III is said to have watched his son, the Black Prince, lead the English army into battle. Drive 6 km. further on to Dompierre-sur-Authie, then turn right on to the D 224, and it is 7 km. to Le Boisle, where you turn left on to the D 928 and drive 17 km. into Hesdin. From 1916 onwards this became an increasingly important British base.

Take the N 39 for Montreuil, 23 km. away.

Montreuil

Once a seaport, Montreuil is an old walled town where narrow streets lead to a large central square in which there is a statue of Field Marshal Haig mounted upon his charger. This is appropriate, because as Commander-in-Chief of the BEF he had his headquarters here from March 1916 to April 1919. Housed mainly in the military college buildings and a variety of temporary accommodations, the staff at HQ probably numbered around 5,000 men of all ranks. Haig himself lived in the Château de Beaurepaire, about 4 km. out of town on the D 138 near Saint-Nicolas, and his residence is marked by a plaque on the gateway.

One of the noisiest units at GHQ must surely have been the messenger-dog service kennels run by the Royal Army Veterinary Corps. In a large enclosure near the town surrounded by a wire fence a

French war dog. Dogs were employed as messengers, scouts, sentinels and trench guards against surprise German attacks. They have been provided with their own trenches in the front line

lone Nissen hut stood amongst some two hundred dog kennels arranged in neat military rows, all equidistant from each other. Dogs came to be extensively used as message-carriers at the front. They could be trained to do the job, and because of their size and speed they were less vulnerable as a target than an orderly or 'runner' bearing a message. Carrier pigeons were used, too – they were especially valuable because they could cover immense distances, presented a minimal target to the enemy, and could fly through clouds of poison gas. In

France in 1918 there was at least one London omnibus in service, which functioned – converted and camouflaged – as a travelling aviary.

Continue on the N 39 for 13 km., mostly beside the River Canche, for Étaples ('Eat Apples' to the BEF).

Étaples

Étaples was an important base and hospital complex that grew from small beginnings in 1915 to become the largest centre for reinforcements in the BEF, with facilities for training around 100,000 men stationed in a series of Infantry Base Depots. In the sand dunes near the station was the notorious 'Bull Ring' where much of the training took place. It is overlooked today by the Étaples Military Cemetery, where 11,000 men of many nations, friend and foe alike, are buried. Today it is the only reminder of what was once a massive military presence.

'A Travelling Aviary'. A London General Omnibus Company bus, still recognizable, used as a travelling aviary for carrier pigeons. Such birds were widely used in the BEF since they could fly through the gas clouds and presented a minimum-sized target to the enemy. This photograph was taken in June 1918

The training staff of the Infantry Base Depots, non-commissioned officers who wore distinguishing yellow armbands and were derisively referred to as 'canaries', gave the men in their charge – whether recruits fresh from Britain or seasoned veterans of the fighting – a very hard time indeed. The latter group were bitterly resentful of this, since few of the 'canaries' seem to have seen active service. To be at Étaples was, recalled one anonymous soldier many years later, 'like passing through hell for two weeks'.[37] Conditions grew so intolerable that in September 1917 there were mass demonstrations in protest at the treatment, and great hostility was shown both to the 'canaries' and to 'red-caps', the military police who were responsible for an oppressive discipline. Within a few days, after much anxiety in high places, things quietened down and the routine at Étaples became less severe.

It was not, however, until 1978 that the government, in answer to a parliamentary question, made any public reference to the mutinies, and then it was simply to say that records had probably been destroyed. In the autumn of 1986 the Étaples mutiny featured in a BBC television series. Several newspapers were outraged by what they saw as a 'left-wing' attempt to rewrite history. The *Daily Mail* in particular was very outspoken; the *Daily Telegraph* was more measured in its response, and in a leading article on 15 September 1986 referred to the BBC's portrayal of events as 'a distortion of a localised incident at a training camp'.

Such a dismissal of what happened at Étaples is misguided. There was, on occasion, unrest in the British army at a number of widely separated locations, even though it was never on the scale of the

French mutinies of 1917; and it is essential for us to understand the strains and tensions, amongst all ranks in the army, engendered by the experience of war. For this reason it is good that such events are beginning to be chronicled in an unsentimental manner.[38] It is just not satisfactory to write of such incidents as 'localised'; nor, on the other hand, is it satisfactory to dismiss those in authority as insensitive bullies. The truth is much more complex, and if we are to find it we must listen attentively to these echoes of a distant tragedy, only part of which was played out here at Étaples.

Continue on the D 940 for Boulogne, 27 km. away, remembering as you go that this is the road along which so many men of the BEF made their way, after landing at Boulogne, by rail or road to Étaples.

Boulogne
An old seaport and well-known holiday centre, Boulogne was used in 1801 as the main base for Napoleon's proposed invasion of the British Isles. More than one hundred years later, on 14 August 1914, the first units of the BEF – commanded in its early days by General Sir John French – began to disembark here; and until the war ended Boulogne remained the chief port of entry for troops coming from Britain.

In the Great War the Germans (except as prisoners of war) did not reach Boulogne; in the Second World War they occupied it and fortified the coast, largely with concrete blockhouses, some of which still remain. During recent years there has been a great deal of building development, and the town has expanded well beyond its 1918 boundaries. Here and there on the outskirts you may see the occasional civilian residence that began life as an army hut.

Leave for Calais on the D 940 and 4 km. from the centre of town reach Terlincthun, where there is a British Military Cemetery. All along these coastal downs there were hospitals and welfare establishments. In 2 km. you come to Wimereux, where 32nd Stationary Hospital, typical of so many others down this coast, was situated. Behind the town cemetery there is a British Communal Cemetery. Because of unstable ground the headstones lie flat; and one of them belongs to Lt-Col. J. M. McCrae, author of 'In Flanders Fields', one of the best-known poems of the Great War.

Continue on the D 940 for a further 36 km., past Cap Gris-Nez, through Wissant to Cap Blanc-Nez with its Dover Patrol Memorial, and finally downhill into Calais.

Calais

This was the chief entry port for all BEF supplies, and a major base with ordnance services, hospitals, training camps, depots and auxiliary units of all kinds. By February 1918 there was a train ferry link with the then newly established Richborough military harbour. As in Boulogne, the occasional military hut survives as a residence.

In 1940 much of Calais was destroyed and the ruins were then surrounded with German fortifications. Now many of these have been removed to make room for new building developments including, of course, the ferry terminal complex, and the result is a totally transformed townscape in which there are few memories or reminders of the Great War. Even the Musée de Guerre (War Museum) in the Parc Saint-Pierre has exhibits mainly related to the conflict of 1939–45.

References

1. Anon., 'The Minor Miseries of War', in *Twenty Years After*, vol. 2, 1938, pp. 1119–20.

2. 'Private 19022', *Her Privates We*, Peter Davies, 1930, p. 388.

3. Robert Graves, *Goodbye to All That*, Penguin Books, 1960 (Jonathan Cape, 1929), pp. 127–8.

4. Guy Chapman, 'An Adjutant Looks Back', in *Twenty Years After*, vol. 1, 1938, p. 563.

5. C. E. Montague, *Disenchantment*, Chatto & Windus, 1922, p. 51.

6. Graves, *op. cit.*, p. 99.

7. John Baynes, *Morale. A Study of Men of Courage*, Cassell, 1967.

8. *ibid.*, p. 82.

9. *ibid.*, p. 82.

10. John Brophy and Eric Partridge, *The Long Trail: The British Army 1914–18*, André Deutsch, 1965, p. 27.

11. Keith Jeffery, 'The Post-War Army', in I. F. W. Beckett and K. Simpson (eds.), *A Nation in Arms*, Manchester University Press, 1985, p. 212.

12. G. Dallas and D. Gill, *The Unknown Army: Mutinies in the British Army in World War I*, Verso, 1985, p. 113.

13. See Andrew Rothstein, *The Soldiers' Strikes of 1919*, Macmillan, 1980, for a well-documented account of these events.

14. *ibid.*, pp. 44–5.

15. A. Pryor and J. K. Woods (eds.), *Great Uncle Fred's War: An Illustrated Diary 1917–20*, Pryor Publications, 1985, p. 54. See also Dallas and Gill, *op. cit.*, chap. 11.

16. Anon., 'A Tommy Looks Back', in *Twenty Years After*, vol. 1, 1938, p. 502.

17. *ibid.*, p. 501.

18. Quoted in Frank Emery (ed.), *Marching Over Africa: Letter from Victorian Soldiers*, Hodder and Stoughton, 1986, p. 176.

19. See *Twenty Years After*, vol. 1, 1938, p. 628.

20. Quoted in Lyn Macdonald, *They Called It Passchendaele*, Michael Joseph, 1978, p. 221.

21. Ernest Parker, *Into Battle 1914–1918*, Longmans, 1976, p. 1.

22. C. J. Arthur, 'A Boy's Experiences', in C. B. Purdom (ed.), *Everyman at War*, Dent, 1930, pp. 176–83.

23. *Twenty Years After*, vol. 2, 1938, p. 1125.

24. See *Twenty Years After*, vol. 3, 1938, p. 210. The British officer concerned, Lt. Spenser, was killed shortly after this episode.

25. There is a good account of Indians on the Western Front in Philip Mason, *A Matter of Honour: An Account of the Indian Army, Its Officers and Men*, Jonathan Cape, 1974, chap. 17.

26. Gerald Brenan, *A Life of One's Own*, Hamish Hamilton, 1962, p. 205.

27. Quoted in R. H. Mottram, *Journey to the Western Front Twenty Years After*, G. Bell, 1936, p. 225.

28. See J. F. C. Fuller, *Tanks in the Great War*, 1920.

29. I am deeply indebted to John Keegan's account of the battle published in David Chandler (ed.), *A Traveller's Guide to the Battlefields of Europe, vol. 1: Western Europe*, 1965, pp. 54–8.

30. *Sir Douglas Haig's Despatches*, Dent, 1979 (1919), p. 155. The German officer was not identified.

31. Marc Ferro, *The Great War 1914–1918*, Routledge, 1973, p. 76.

32. *ibid.*

33. Captain A. J. Dawson, *For France*, 1917, pp. 165–6. The book was illustrated by Captain Bruce Bairnsfather.

34. J. A. Hayward, 'A Casualty Clearing Station', in Purdom (ed.), *op. cit.*

35. See *Twenty Years After*, vol. 3, 1938, p. 246.

36. Told by CQMS G. W. Fisher, 1st Batt. Herts. Regt, in Macdonald, *op. cit.*, pp. 121–2.

37. Quoted in Dallas and Gill, *op. cit.*, p. 65.

38. Dallas and Gill, *op. cit.* See also Rothstein, *op. cit.*

Some Background Reading

The literature of the Great War is endless, and the titles offered here are included because each one will enhance, in some way or another, a visit to the Western Front. Each, all or a selection of these books can equally well be read before, during or after a visit to the battlefields.

Some of the earliest guidebooks, though long out of print, are well worth looking for in second-hand bookshops, or could be consulted in a few libraries. In the years immediately following the Armistice, Michelin, the famous French tyre company, with an office in the Fulham Road, London, issued a series in English entitled *Illustrated Michelin Guides to the Battle-Fields (1914–1918)*. With plenty of photographs and maps, they convey a vivid sense of what the landscape looked like when the war ended. The volume on Ypres and the two volumes on the Somme are extremely good. Outstanding, however, among these older guides is Finlay Muirhead, *Belgium and the Western Front*, published jointly by Macmillan, London, and Hachette, Paris, in 1920. It is one of the celebrated Blue Guides, and while it does not have any photographs, the coloured folding maps and general coverage of the war make it, despite its age, a valuable and readable reference book. There are altogether sixty maps and plans, together with a succinct account of the British campaigns in the west written by General Sir F. D. Maurice. Published in 1938 and edited by General Sir Ernest Swinton, the three substantial volumes of *Twenty*

Years After. The Battlefields of 1914–1918. Then and Now, though hardly a guide, are well worth consulting. Both the illustrations and the accompanying text are fascinating, informative and compulsive.

Other more readily available titles include the following:

For the Sake of Example. Capital Courts Martial 1914–1918
Babington, Anthony
Leo Cooper/Secker & Warburg, 1983, and *Paladin Books,* 1985
Essential reading for an understanding of the military mind. The author, himself a judge, is the first writer to have been given access to official Ministry of Defence files on these cases.

A Military Atlas of the First World War
Banks, Arthur
Heinemann, 1975
Very clearly drawn maps. As the title indicates, they are not confined to the Western Front.

A Nation in Arms
Beckett, I. F. W. *and* Simpson, K. (ed.)
Manchester University Press, 1985
Subtitled *A Social Study of the British Army in the First World War,* this collection of essays represents a pioneer study of the army and the society from which it was drawn.

Before Endeavours Fade. A Guide to the Battlefields of the First World War
Coombs, Rose E. B.
After the Battle, 1976, and *Battle of Britain Print* (5th edn), 1986
The standard guide, thorough and reliable. A little too detailed, perhaps, for the casual tourist, and no concessions are made to those with little knowledge of the organization and ranks of the army.

The Unknown Army. Mutinies in the British Army in World War 1
Dallas, G.

and Gill,   *Verso*, 1985
     D.   A compelling account of mutiny and insubordination, a theme about which little has been written, this book provides some valuable and incisive perspectives on the occasional clashes between militant sections of the working class serving as soldiers and the military machine.

Dunn,   **The War the Infantry Knew. A Chronicle of Service**
J. C.   **in France and Belgium**
     Jane's, 1987
     First published in a limited edition (P. S. King, 1938) and now reprinted, this is one of the most revealing books about the experiences of one infantry battalion on the Western Front.

Ferro,   **The Great War 1914–1918**
Marc   *Routledge*, 1973
     An excellent one-volume history of the war.

Graves,   **Goodbye to All That**
Robert   *Penguin*, 1960
     Lively, authentic and admirably written account of the author's experiences with the Royal Welch Fusiliers.

Jones,   **The War Walk. A Journey Along the Western**
Nigel H.   **Front**
     Robert Hale, 1983
     A lively account of a 400-mile walk along the line of the old trenches.

Liddell Hart,   **History of the First World War**
B. H.   *Pan Books*, 1972
     First published as *The Real War 1914–1918* (Faber, 1930), a standard work, always readable, sometimes contentious

Macdonald,   **They Called It Passchendaele**
Lyn   *Macmillan*, 1983, and *Michael Joseph*, 1978
     Somme
     Macmillan, 1984, and *Michael Joseph*, 1983

Vivid accounts of two battles, drawing heavily and effectively upon the testimonies of survivors.

The First Day on the Somme. 1st July 1916 Middlebrook,
Allen Lane, 1971, and *Penguin Books*, 1984 Martin
Brilliant reconstruction of the opening day of the battle.

✓ **Men Who March Away** Parsons,
Chatto & Windus, 1965, 1978, *Heinemann*, 1965, 1979, I. M.
and *Hogarth Press*, 1987
A much reprinted anthology of First World War poetry.

The First World War Robbins,
Oxford University Press, 1984, 1985 Keith
An excellent brief survey.

The Soldiers' Strikes of 1919 Rothstein,
Macmillan, 1980 A.
A vivid account by one who took part. This book was probably the first to examine such themes as insubordination. A necessary perspective on the war and its aftermath.

Four Years on the Western Front, by a Rifleman Smith,
London Stamp Exchange, 1988 Aubrey
First published, anonymously, in 1922 (Odhams Press), this is a vivid account of the war as seen through the eyes of a man in the ranks of the London Rifle Brigade

The First World War. An Illustrated History Taylor,
Hamish Hamilton, 1963, and *Penguin Books*, 1970 A. J. P.
Trenchant and, as one might suspect, never dull.

Death's Men. Soldiers of the Great War Winter,
Allen Lane, 1978, and *Penguin Books*, 1979 Denis
Outstandingly good. Describes what it was like to be a soldier on the Westen Front.

Index